KT-174-442

A Parrish Affair

ORLA KELLY
PUBLISHING

Tessa Daly

978-1-912328-60-4

© 2020 by Tessa Daly. All rights reserved.

This book is copyright under the Berne Convention. All intellectual property rights including copyright, design right and publishing rights rest with the author. No part of this book may be reproduced or transmitted in any way including any written, electronic, recording, or photocopying without written permission of the author. This is entirely a work of fiction. Names, characters, businesses, places, events, locales, and incidents are either the products of the author's imagination or used in a fictitious manner. Any resemblance to actual persons, living or dead, or actual events is purely coincidental. Edited by Red Pen Edits Published by Orla Kelly Publishing. Cover design by Jordan Daly Photography.

Orla Kelly Publishing
Kilbrody,
Mount Oval,
Rochestown,
Cork,
Ireland

Acknowledgements

This book would not have happened without Orla Kelly Self-Publishing Services. From the time I made contact with Orla, she was there for me all the way. Thanks Orla.

Thank you, also to my friend Orla Morrissey, who encouraged me to keep going.

To my nephew Jay, of Jordan Daly Photography for the photo and for your art work on the cover. Thanks Jordan.

BAINTE DEN STOC

WITHDRAWN FROM DLR LIBRARIES STOCK

Contents

Chapter 1

Monday morning and Ciara Parrish was happy and content as she drove the short distance to her office, which was adjacent to the local national school and just a short walk from the Catholic Church in the townland of Ballyfauna, County Wicklow.

She had no idea that this day was one that she would never forget.

The school was just closed for the summer holidays. There were another seven weeks to go before she got her summer break. She liked the quietness of the schoolyard at this time, knowing that she could get on with her work without interruption. She could even put a CD in the player. During this time, she could wear casual clothes and did not bother with make-up.

Ciara Connolly grew up in County Tipperary along with her sister, Kate. Their parents died tragically when they were very young children, and they were brought up by their father's older sister, a single woman they called Auntie. Their aunt looked after all their basic needs; they were always well-dressed and fed the best of food. The girls knew from watching their friends interact with their parents that they had missed out on the love of a mother and father. They saw this when they went to visit their friend's houses, but their aunt never let them have kids visit their home, and as children, they never understood this.

On her deathbed, Auntie wished that they would have good lives and find love and happiness, the sort she had never had or been able to give them, but she hoped that she had done enough for them. They were two young adults now, and the rest was up to them.

Later the two girls discussed her words and wondered if they were the reason that Auntie had not found love in her life. Now they would never know.

This was to shape the rest of their lives. Kate decided to become a psychologist, as she was interested in understanding the human condition, the differences between them and the other children she had watched growing up in close-knit family units. On the other hand, Ciara just wanted a family of her own – almost to the point of being obsessive and was not driven to succeed in any particular field. It was what she dreamed about as a young girl and what she still wanted. A good and faithful husband who wanted children and a quiet family life, like the one that they had missed out on. That was her only goal, and as she listened to her friends planning their careers and their travel plans, she was aware that none of them included marriage or children. She didn't mention it either, fearing that they would make fun of her.

When she finished secondary school, her aunt was happy to allow her to get a job as a junior in a legal office in Dublin instead of insisting on her going to college. For this Ciara was grateful because after Kate left for college, she felt very much alone with only her maiden aunt for company.

Ciara was now the secretary for both the local school and church. She had plenty to do, but it was not as taxing as the work she had done in the legal office in Dublin, where she had worked until she married the love of her life, Bill Parrish. She fell head over heels in love with him the first day he walked into the office. With his dark straight hair, long at the front but perfectly cut and groomed, he was at least six foot three and very well-built. She had never met such a handsome man. All the girls swooned when he was in the office. Ciara had laughed along with them. He had concluded his business with the solicitor and left, taking care to say goodbye to Ciara using her first name; she assumed this was as it was on her name tag.

About an hour after he had left the office, she answered the phone. She recognised his voice straight away. "Hello Mr Parrish, how can I help you?" Having thought it was a business call Ciara was a little confused when she realised that he was asking her to lunch that very day. "But Mr Parrish – sorry, Bill. We know nothing about each other."

He cut in immediately. "That is the point of meeting. I would like to get to know you. So, how about meeting me for lunch?"

They met at a restaurant close to the office an hour later. After which, he walked her back to the office. "Can we do this again?" Bill asked. Ciara couldn't believe that he had asked her out and not one of the other girls who were much more glamorous than her. It was difficult to concentrate on work that afternoon as thoughts of Bill Parrish kept coming to mind. Ciara felt a bit giddy.

Following that first lunch, Bill phoned her every day. Sometimes he made the trip from Wicklow town just to have lunch with her, which was very flattering. No man had ever made such a fuss of her before. To her delight, he was pleasant company and they chatted easily. When they walked into a restaurant or bar, people looked. Ciara felt ten feet tall and was grateful that they were not looking at her but the man at her side.

It was very different from being asked out to a club. Then having to fend off a man afterwards when she was not in the least bit attracted to him, having spent only a few hours in his company listening to him talking about himself, and him not wanting to know anything about her or her life.

Bill was the opposite, he was interested in every aspect of her life and only talked about himself when she asked about his life and work. They realised that they had common interests, as they both came from the countryside and loved everything about it. Neither of them had any family to speak of. He had some distant cousins in America, but none he was close to. Ciara also had cousins, but no immediate relations apart from Kate. As their relationship grew, Ciara realised that she was in love with this man and couldn't wait for their next meeting or phone call. She liked his voice and was happy just listening to him talk about his hopes for the future, which were just like her own.

They went for long walks in the Wicklow mountains and ate in some of the best restaurants in Wicklow. They went to shows in Dublin. On occasion, they went out with Kate and her husband, Marcus Langley.

It was every girl's dream, a whirlwind romance with the proverbial tall, dark and handsome man. Six months after their first meeting, Bill proposed to her while having dinner at one of the best restaurants in Dublin. Ciara didn't hesitate to say yes. This was, after all, all she had ever wanted and more. Bill had his own business and a big house in the country and was not interested in clubbing or any of the things that other young men were into. He didn't look at or admire other girls, he only wanted to be with her.

Chapter 2

Ayear later, they were married. It was not a big wedding, just a small gathering of a few friends and colleagues. Ciara expected Bill to invite some of his neighbours as he was brought up in the parish and surely must know a lot of people there, but he explained that he had gone to boarding school and lost contact with the local people.

Kate was the bridesmaid, and Marcus stood with Bill at the church in Ballyfauna. A reception was held at Bill's ancestral home and now her home, Ivy Manor. All the food was provided by caterers. The wine and champagne flowed for many hours. Ciara's friends said that she was the luckiest woman alive to be living in such a grand house with a man as attentive as Bill. Yes, she thought so too.

Ciara had given up her job and apartment in Dublin to live in Ballyfauna. Bill wanted her to take up a position in the family business. However, common sense told her that this was not a good idea and may not be the best for their marriage. She had talked about this with Kate, and she had agreed.

Finding a job locally was her best option. She couldn't believe her luck when visiting the local shop, a woman told her that a secretary was needed at the local primary school. The woman asked if she was interested and offered to put her name forward for the job.

Bill was not impressed. He said that with her experience as a legal secretary, she would be wasting her time at the local school. By this time Ciara knew that her husband was a bit of a snob and she laughed quietly to herself as she explained how nice it would be if they had a child in the school with her working there. Ciara also wanted to get to know her neighbours. Their children would have friends growing up, and they would come to Ivy Manor to play – she would not isolate them. When she put this idea to her husband, she saw a change in his face. Then it softened again.

"But darling, our children will go to boarding school," he said, as if it were the most natural thing in the world. He crossed the floor and put his arm around her shoulder like you would if you were trying to pacify a child.

"Boarding school? No. Bill, you must be joking. No child of mine will be sent away from home until they are ready to go to college." It was Ciara's turn to be outraged.

Bill was wise enough to pull back from this argument for now. He left it looking like his wife had the last word, but it was a Parrish tradition, and his children would be going the same way. Bill always got his way.

Chapter 3

Fifteen minutes into her day, there was a loud knock on her office door. She turned around to get out of her chair to answer the door but before she could reach it, it opened. A man entered the office. She shook the outstretched hand.

"Father David Magee. I believe you are expecting me."

"Oh! Father Magee," stammered Ciara. "Yes, I knew that you were to arrive soon. I had no idea that it was to be today." She was about to ask him to have a seat but didn't have time. He was already sitting. There was nothing formal about this man.

He sat back in a chair and looked around, as if memorising the entire contents of the office, then turned his attention to Ciara. "So, you are the Mrs Parrish who runs the parish of Ballyfauna," he said. A broad grin crept across his face. Ciara opened her mouth to protest but he didn't wait for her to say anything. "Well," he continued, still smiling, "I have it from a good source that you are the backbone of this place and that I need to be nice to you if I want to get things done." He was laughing now, and she was just a bit uncomfortable with the way he was so comfortable having just come through the door for the first time. She felt that he could see through her, read her mind.

Ciara stood up to hide her discomfort, wishing now that she was in a bigger space. "It is nice to meet you, Father Magee. While I don't actually run the parish, I do my best at my job," she said trying to sound professional.

"Well, it is good to meet you, Mrs Parrish," said Father Magee.

"Ciara, please Father."

He also stood up and put his hand out again. They shook hands and he seemed to hold onto her hand a little longer than usual. "As we are to be work colleagues, call me David, ok?" He handed her a card with his phone number on it. "Ring me if you need anything. Mind you, it will probably be me ringing you." He then turned to the door.

Ciara found herself following him out and noticed that he was almost as tall as Bill and well-built. She held the door open as he left and watched as he went down the steps. She went back inside and sat in her chair. What the hell had just happened, she thought.

The new parish priest was not what she expected him to be. He struck her as a man first, then a priest. He was very confident, but not in an arrogant sense. He was a far cry from the last priest. Father O'Driscoll was an old man, and he had left most things to Ciara. He was not one for change unless it was absolutely essential. Things might be different around here, if first impressions are anything to go by.

Try as she might, Ciara was unable to get back to what she started, there were so many things going on in her head. There was something about this man, but she didn't know what it was. When her phone rang, it was a very welcome distraction, especially when she realised it was her sister Kate.

"Hi sis, how is life with you today?" said Kate when she answered the call.

"Good," said Ciara as she sighed deeply.

"What is that sigh about? Are you under pressure or something?"

"I just met the new parish priest. I am still trying to imagine what things are going to be like around here, with him as the boss," said Ciara.

"Oh, go on! Do tell me – what is he like? Is he tall, dark and handsome or what?"

"Let me put it this way, Kate, he is nothing like what I am used to. Seems very confident, but in a relaxed sort of way. He is tall, going slightly grey and while he couldn't compete with my husband in the looks department, neither is he ugly," she said as she threw her head back and laughed with her sister.

Kate said, "Let's just hope he is good to work with. Are you and Bill doing anything for the weekend?"

"We have no plans as far as I know. Unless Bill has something planned. Why do you ask?" said Ciara.

"Why don't you both come up to us and we can go to the Curragh on Saturday?"

Ciara didn't need to think about this. She loved spending time with her sister. "Sounds good. I will check with Bill tonight – not that he ever turned down a day at the races! Plus, he can't wait to show off his new shiny black jeep!" The two women laughed.

That night Bill rang Marcus to confirm that they would be there Saturday. Bill did not make friends easily. The Connolly sisters were glad that their husbands got on very well. Let's face it, if they didn't, the girls could not meet as often.

It was not the easy week that Ciara had hoped for, with the arrival of Father Magee, who had to be brought up to speed on all aspects of the parish. There were lots of phone calls and messages, some of them after working hours. She could sense Bill becoming impatient, but he said nothing.

Not all the time they spent in the office was work. They chatted easily, and he talked about himself and enquired about Ciara and her life. She even took an extra portion of lunch with her in case he was there at lunchtime. During this time the mood was light, and Father Magee also told a few jokes. He assured her that she would be reimbursed for lunch and extra hours.

This new working relationship seemed to be going well to Ciara's great relief. She would hate to have to leave her job and go to work in town if she couldn't get on with him. Instead she found herself looking forward to the time they spent together. Bill still wanted her to work for him, but she was sticking to her guns. She liked getting to know the teachers and some of the parents, and for the first time in her life, she felt at home.

Friday lunchtime came. It was time to go and pack for the weekend. She would just check in with Father David, to remind him that she was leaving early.

"Ok, Ciara. Thanks for all your help. Have a good time."

Ciara couldn't resist saying, "If you have any questions, call me. Bye, David."

Bill was already at home when Ciara got there. He had prepared lunch for her and was sitting at the breakfast bar as they rarely used the dining room. He came towards his wife with a big smile on his face. He put his arms around her and kissed her passionately.

"Luncheon is served, madam," he said in a low voice. They kissed again and Ciara nodded towards stairs. Holding hands, they both ran to the bedroom.

"Come on, let's make a baby," laughed Bill, as they both undressed.

Ciara loved having sex with her husband, but right now there seemed to be an urgency about it, which made it less enjoyable. She wished he would think of just loving her and not always talking about making a baby.

They were both in good form, as they set out for Naas, to spend the weekend with Kate and Marcus. The husbands got on very well and shared a love of horse racing. Neither was a big gambler, but they enjoyed a flutter and all the banter that went with a day at the track. For the sisters, it was time together and a chance to get dressed up, not to mention looking at the style all around them.

Fifteen minutes into the journey, Ciara's phone rang. "David?" answered Ciara. "What can I do for you?" The conversation lasted for about four minutes, and she could feel the tension coming from her husband.

When the call ended, he looked across at her and said, "Well, what did he want or is he missing you already?" There was no hint of humour in the question, just sarcasm.

"He just needed some answers, and I am the only person who could help him. No big deal," said Ciara.

Bill was just beginning to relax when the phone rang again.

"David, that's ok. No problem, I am just sitting in the jeep. Bill is driving," Ciara answered the parish priest's question and said goodbye.

Now, Bill was no longer irritated, he was clearly angry. "Why the hell is he ringing you on your time off? This is our time. You are not working now. Turn your damn phone off and let him ring someone else!"

In all the time they had been together, he had never before given her an order, but this was an order.

"Hold on now," said Ciara. "Father Magee is my boss and will be for a long time to come. I told him to ring me if he needed to, same as Father O'Driscoll before him. You never complained before, why now? What is your problem, Bill?"

"He is my fucking problem. I don't like him."

"But he has only been here a week, and you haven't even met the man. How can you dislike him?"

With no real answer for his feelings about Father David Magee, at least nothing that he was ready to share with his wife, Bill decided to say no more. Ciara did not turn her phone off, and David did not ring again before they arrived at their destination.

As they drove into the driveway at Marcus and Kate's, Bill reached over and caught Ciara's hand. He looked at her with pleading in his eyes and said, "I'm sorry, sweetheart. Forgive me for being such a fool?"

Ciara was cross at him but decided to let it go. "OK," she said but yet something had changed.

Chapter 4

Marcus was out of his front door and opening the car door for Ciara. He always welcomed them into his house, as if it was their first visit. The Langley's lived in a bungalow in a built-up area but they had plenty space for parking. The place was well-kept because they had someone come in to do it for them.

There was just one thing that niggled at Bill about Marcus and Kate, their decision not to have children. He could not get his head around this. Marcus was a surgeon and Kate a psychologist at the same hospital. They would make great parents, and they could afford to pay someone to look after the kids.

He had had this conversation several times with Ciara, and she always said the same. "It's their choice. Children are not compulsory in a marriage."

He always answered. "But you do want a family, don't you?" It always appeared more like a command than a question.

"Yes, my darling, I do. And it will happen. When the time is right, the baby will come. We are still young, Bill. We have plenty of time for kids. Let's just enjoy our life together."

Marcus stood back, admiring the new jeep. "When did you get it?"

"During the week," answered Bill. "What do you think?" The two men spent at least fifteen minutes, admiring the new purchase. Marcus Langley didn't care much about material things. He loved Kate, his job and their modest home. When they were both off duty at the same time, they liked to do some gardening and shop for unusual little things for the house.

Kate just had one look at her younger sister to know that something was wrong. "Come on, sis. Let's put your bags in the bedroom and you can tell me what is wrong." They sat on the end of the bed and Ciara started to cry. Kate didn't try to stop her. She let her tell all about her husband and his attitude to her new boss.

"I don't know what his problem is. They haven't even met, but he has a real bee in his bonnet about Father David. If he keeps going, I will lose my job. You know that I was always there for the last parish priest – at his beck and call, you might say. But Kate, that is the job, and I have no problem with it."

Kate put her arm around her sister and in a gentle voice asked, "Could he be jealous of him?"

"What?" Ciara almost shouted. "What makes you say that?"

"Sorry. Just thinking out loud. You know what some men are like. They need all your attention."

"Yes, and he has that, except for my job. It's the way it has always been, but now he gets upset if I get a phone call at home."

"There is just one difference, Ciara. Your new boss from what you tell me, is not a bit like his predecessor. Now cheer up and let us enjoy the weekend. Now let me see what you are going to wear tomorrow. I don't want to look like the poor relation beside you."

Ciara pulled a smart red and white dress from her bag with shoes and a bag to match it.

"Wow. That is lovely. Come on, it's my turn."

They went to Marcus and Kate's room and went through the wardrobe to make sure they didn't clash. Kate picked out pale pink pants and matched it with a navy top. "Perfect. Now, it's time for a glass of wine." They walked along the narrow hallway to join the men in the kitchen. Unlike Ivy Manor, Langley's house was more homely, and the kitchen was the centre of the home. There was no formal dining room. They went from the kitchen to the living room, and they were both very comfortable rooms that reflected the people who live there.

Marcus opened a bottle of red and a bottle of white wine. He poured four glasses. Then took Ciara by the arm. "Come on, young lady. I have something to show you. It's a Mark Bradford."

Bill looked questioningly at Kate.

"A new painting," said Kate. "He loves showing it off." They both laughed.

The painting was beautiful, and Ciara could have stayed there just looking at it for a long time but her phone rang. Ciara took the call, and Marcus joined his wife and Bill in the kitchen. Marcus nodded back towards his study. "Ciara got a phone call."

Kate immediately noticed how her brother-in-law reacted and how his handsome face changed as he ran his fingers through his dark hair. She was sure that it was jealousy he was showing, and she wondered why. He was not the sort of man to pour his heart out; all she could do was say, "More wine, Bill?" She had not seen this side of him before and was really surprised to find a confident and good-looking man like Bill react like this about a priest who works with his wife. Ciara came back in, and Kate served up dinner. As she did it, she was worried. They always seemed like the perfect couple. People would say they had it all. But in her work, Kate found that not many people had it all and jealousy was never good in a marriage. After dinner, the form book came out and the mood settled. The two couples sat opposite each other. Bill and Ciara looked as if nothing could come between them. They discussed horses, trainers and jockeys for The Curragh the next day. The husbands laughed as their wives talked about what the men should wear. You couldn't be overdressed for The Curragh racecourse. Kate picked out clothes for Marcus. She said that he would go in his scrubs if it were up to him. The four of them laughed. The evening was a real pleasure.

Kate, in her wisdom, decided that it was not a good idea to talk about the new priest over this weekend, as neither one of them were at the point of admitting that there was a problem. They would enjoy their time together and hopefully it would work out for them. She loved them both and wanted them to be happy.

Father Magee was not mentioned again. However, while at The Curragh the next day Kate noticed her sister answering her phone. From her reaction, Kate guessed who the call was from. While totally unaware of it, Ciara had a look of excitement on her face. She talked and giggled like a schoolgirl. Bill and Marcus were off looking at the runners for the next race, which was just as well. She realised now that Bill was jealous for a reason, even if her sister was in denial.

Chapter 5

Bill loved his job running Parrish & Son Accountants. The business had been started by his grandfather when he arrived in Wicklow from America in the late 1940s. Bill's father took over from his father, and hopefully, it would continue into the next generation. His grandfather also built the Georgian style house complete with conservatory and named it, Ivy Manor. It was the only big house in the area not put there by the British.

As an only son, Bill always knew what he was going to do with his life. He would go to university, become an accountant and run the family business, live in Ivy Manor with a wife and children. He was good at school and never had problems with girls, got on well with both sexes and was considered a good catch. He had known and gone out with a few girls while in university and just after that, but no one that he believed to be wife material.

It was not long after that he met Ciara Connolly. Bill had immediately known that he had met his future wife. She had all the qualities that he was looking for. She was the first girl that he took home. He hadn't known Ciara very long when he mentioned marriage – he did not want this girl to get away. She was everything he could want – beautiful, smart, down to earth, very sociable and he couldn't wait to marry her. She was not the sort of girl who would marry for money or status, and he had lots of both. He considered himself a fortunate man. Apart, from the loss of his mother at a young age and then much later, his father. Bill hadn't seen hardship in his life.

For Bill, a baby would be the icing on the cake, then he would have it all – the business, the wife, the house and a child. What else could a man want? In his mind, he really wanted a son to carry on the business and the Parrish name. This he kept to himself though.

They rarely went out, unless it was to the rugby club in town, and then they had to get a taxi home. There was a friendly pub in Ballyfauna, which they could walk to and they did from time to time, but it was just a chance to meet their neighbours and have a chat. Bill was a big fish in a small pond. When they did visit the local pub, the local men sought him out. They hung on his every word. The women liked him too. Ciara guessed that a few of them might have imagined themselves living at Ivy Manor, with the tall dark and handsome accountant. Wasn't she lucky to have married such a catch!

Chapter 6

Much of her time at the office in the coming weeks was in the company of Father Magee. She liked him, and they worked well together. Her desk always had just one seat in front of the computer; now it had two, side by side with not much space between them. David was a regular in the office. They both laughed as Ciara pointed out things about people that David was better off knowing if he did not want to say the wrong things to people he would encounter while working in a place as small as Ballyfauna.

"What I was told about being nice to you, Ciara Parrish, was right. Just imagine if I didn't know all this stuff!"

"Who told you that anyway?" said Ciara, laughing.

"Oh, you know how people talk."

"I do. I know well, and you are better off not listening to most of it."

"Yes, Mrs Parrish," he said, in mock seriousness.

As she reached across the desk for a pen, David also moved. Their hands momentarily touched. It was like a spark of electricity passing between them. They both pulled back as if bitten by something. They looked at each other for an instant unable to find words. Then the moment passed when David put his hand out to get the pen, "This one?"

"Yes, please," answered Ciara, and she could still feel the touch of his hand as if it had burned into her skin. With some difficulty, she carried on working.

David liked working with Ciara. She was a breath of fresh air compared to some secretaries he had to get along with in the past. There was something beautiful and innocent about her. He had never looked at a woman like that before. He knew that he had no business doing so now, but he couldn't help it. Just sitting there with her, chatting and laughing was a totally new experience for him. He looked forward to meeting her most days. He could never admit to it, but sometimes he made up excuses to go to the office when a phone call would have done. Still, he was not doing any harm or so he told himself. Ciara was happily married, and he was committed to the church.

David rarely wore clerical wear, unless he had official duties to perform. Mostly he wore casual shirts and pants, and Ciara couldn't really see him in the same way that she had Father O'Driscoll. She felt comfortable in his company, and it never crossed her mind to call him Father anymore. Continuing to wear her casual clothes she felt relaxed, but she did take a little extra care when getting ready for work. Not being used to having another person at her desk, let alone having a man sitting that close to her. She wore a subtle perfume and some light foundation. They were just two people working well together and enjoying each other's company, she reminded herself.

Ciara decided that it was time to ask David to meet her husband, but when she put it to Bill, he brushed the idea aside. "I'm sure I will meet him soon enough."

"Oh, well, if you are not prepared to even meet the man, you can't say that you don't like him."

With just another week to work before they went to Tramore Races with Kate and Marcus, Ciara had a lot to do before the school reopened. There was no one to take her place when she had time off and to make things more difficult she had her period. This always made her feel like curling up in bed and right now she was not looking forward to the week at the racetrack.

Bill, on the other hand, was full of the joys of life, except for the fact that his wife was not pregnant. He made himself busy in the evenings, laying out clothes for himself and Ciara. Bill took great care of himself and was always well-dressed. He knew her so well that he could choose her clothes and he did this while she was curled up in front of the TV with a heat pack on her stomach.

The first race meeting was not until Thursday, but the group decided to go down on Monday and enjoy the beach and the excellent food in the area, generally laze around and do some sightseeing. There were a lot of new attractions in the sunny southeast since they were there last. They could visit Waterford Castle; the men would enjoy the golf and the girls would have no problem filling in their time exploring the grounds.

The night before they were due to travel, Bill did a checklist. It was all written down, to the last detail. He rang Johnny, who looked after the garden and general maintenance of the house, to make sure that he would be in tomorrow and check in every day for the week that they were away.

After that, he looked to his wife. "Now, I want no calls from that priest while we are on holiday, ok?"

Ciara didn't know if she should laugh or cry. She smiled and said, "I will turn my phone off. Just to please you, darling. Ok? But when we get back, I want you to meet Father Magee. I think you will get on well together. Will you do that for me, please Bill?"

Agreeing, Ciara breathed a sigh of relief.

Chapter 7

When they arrived at the Majestic Hotel, they were pleasantly surprised. It very grand. They got parking right outside the hotel. Marcus had made the booking. They should have known that he would pick one of the best hotels around.

Hotel rooms were much the same wherever you went. What made this one different was the view. The Atlantic Ocean took Ciara's breath away and she couldn't wait to go and see the beach. There was also a garden to be explored, but that would have to wait. Bill had other ideas. He wanted to try out the bed.

"Later, darling," said Ciara as she made for the door. She waited for him to join her, but he didn't seem interested.

"You go. I will unpack."

Relief flooded through Ciara as she left the hotel. They had a good sex life until recently, but now he seemed more interested in making a baby than he was in her. She had told him how she felt, but he appeared not to hear her.

Ciara felt lonely as she left the hotel. It looks like her husband was only interested in making her pregnant. As she made her way to the prom, it became clear in her mind that the best sex they ever had was before they got married.

Oh my God, was that Bill's only interest in her? Did he choose her to be the mother to his heir? She needed to sit down. Fortunately, there was a lot of seating on the street. She sat down. Her head was spinning. Why didn't she see this before, what was wrong with her?

'Does he love me? Did he ever love me? What am I going to do now? Maybe I am just being stupid. It is that time of the month, after all. And hormones can play tricks with the mind. Yes, that's it. Now walk on and enjoy the view,' Ciara said to herself.

The promenade in Tramore was packed with people just walking and enjoying the sea air. The sounds of the amusements gave the place a real holiday feeling. Not something that she would like every day, but right now it was good. There were families heading into the sea and old people sitting there taking it all in. Ciara found another vacant seat and sat down. She couldn't shake the feeling that her husband was more interested in making a baby than he was in making love with her.

They had said that they would still have great sex when they were old and grey. Now they were only one year into the marriage, and he was obsessed with having a baby. However, they were here to enjoy themselves, and now she would take in the atmosphere and not think about her marriage anymore for today. When she was ready, she decided that a walk on the beach would be nice.

She stood up and turned to the left, to walk to the far end of the prom. What she saw coming towards her, knocked her for six. It was Father David Magee and a woman. He was in black, complete with dog collar. The woman looked younger. That was all she could see before she turned back to the right and tried to become invisible.

He didn't see her. He just walked past and continued chatting to the woman at his side. The woman was tall, slender and well-dressed, about Ciara's age, she thought. What was he doing here? And who was the woman?

She went back and sat down again. Ciara had no idea how long she sat there. Her heart was racing. She felt like she had seen a ghost. What did it matter to her? And why didn't she just meet him and say hello? She felt foolish about this. These questions began to frighten her. Was her husband right? Did she have a crush on the parish priest? It was as if the gods were laughing at her. Her with her perfect life now having to question her marriage and her job. What next?

Chapter 8

The sun had gone behind the cloud and she was suddenly cold. She picked herself up and decided that she was just stupid, because of how Bill was acting and Kate's suggestion that her husband was somehow jealous of Father Magee spending time in her company at work.

'Enough of this. I will go back to the hotel now and forget all about it. Marcus and Kate should have arrived by this time.' Her thoughts straightened out as she turned back towards the hotel.

On the short walk, she received a text from her sister. 'Where are you? We are in the bar with Bill. Come and join us.'

Ciara replied to the text, 'On my way.' She needed a stiff drink.

As she entered the bar, she could see the three of them sitting at the far end of the bar. 'They all looked very glamorous,' she thought. Kate, with her short blonde hair pushed pack behind one ear, dressed in pale pink and Marcus, while not as tall as Bill, was indeed a very attractive man in a light blue shirt. Bill in a blue and red check shirt, stood out as the most handsome man in the bar but he stood out no matter what he wore. Kate waved to her, and she started to walk towards them.

As she walked through the bar, she heard a voice call out to her. Was she dreaming? Suddenly there he was, heading in her direction. She felt overwhelmed but somehow managed to compose herself enough to say "Father Magee, how are you?"

They shook hands quickly. Though he talked, she could not hear him. She was fully aware that she was being watched very closely from across the room. "Come and meet my family," said Ciara, hoping that this awkward moment could be turned around. She led the way, and he followed her accompanied by the young woman. "This is my husband, Bill Parrish. Bill, meet Father David Magee."

"Pleased to meet you, Bill," said David shaking his hands.

She didn't hear what Bill answered. "This is my sister Kate and her husband Marcus Langley." David shook hands all around. It was Marcus who did most of the talking after that.

"You sound like a Cork man, Father," said Marcus.

"Yes, I am."

"As am I!" said Marcus.

They chatted easily. Ciara was shell-shocked, and even though her sister was speaking to her, she didn't hear a word, let alone notice that the woman had joined their company.

David touched her arm gently, and she looked around. "Ciara," he said gently, "I would like you to meet my sister, Mary." Ciara took the outstretched hand and shook it. It was warm and firm. Mary had a beautiful smile, and Ciara liked her instantly. She felt mortified. What sort of a man did she think David was? He was after all a priest!

It was Mary who began the conversation. "So, you are the lady who took my big brother in hand and showed him the lay of the new job."

"Yes," Bill said, "my wife is very good at what she does. Dedicated, you might say." Was there a slight touch of sarcasm in that tone Ciara wondered?

"Oh, Bill! This is Mary."

"Yes, we have just been introduced. What brings you to Tramore, Mary?" asked Bill now with a hint of a smile.

"Well, I was coming down for the races with friends and my brother came here to meet me. We don't get many chances to meet up. I am delighted to meet you both. I'm very glad that he has friends in Ballyfauna. It can be a very lonely life being a priest, moving from one part of the country to another."

Bill nodded and moved away to the counter calling for another drink. 'More to get out of any further conversation,' thought Ciara. He had made no attempt to talk to or get to know David.

Kate was watching things play out and decided to go to Bill's rescue. Though he was smiling, Kate could see that he was furious.

"Did he know that we were coming here?" he said to Kate, through gritted teeth.

"Now Bill, that is just crazy. Marcus told you last night that he had only just booked this hotel. How could Father Magee possibly have known? What is your problem, Bill?" Kate had moved him away from the rest of the company. "He seems like a nice man to me. Ciara works well with him. Surely you want a happy wife to come home to. Don't you?"

Bill said nothing for a few minutes. Then he looked his sister-in-law straight in the face. "Kate, I know my wife. I have watched her on the phone talking to that man. Priest or no priest, her face lights up when she is talking to him. If you were taking notice of her, as a professional, you would see it too." Bill Parrish was many things, but he was not a fool.

Kate knew that it was futile, but she attempted to diffuse the situation. "Ciara is simply delighted she has a boss that she can get on with, and maybe have a joke with, that she smiles when talking to him. Men and women can be friends, you know. Bill, you two are solid. Stop worrying, or you just might drive her away. Many marriages have failed because of a jealous partner. You need to get it under control, and soon."

Though a faint smile passed his lips, it did not extend to his eyes. "Come on let's go and have some fun" was all Kate could say.

David and Marcus were still chatting, as were Ciara and Mary. They were all unaware of the turmoil that was going on in Bill's head. Kate could only guess what it was. She went to join her husband and the priest to see what sort of man Father Magee was. He moved back to allow her to take a seat at the bar.

"So, you two Cork men are getting on well then?" she joked. Typically, they all laughed. "Are you not having a drink, Father Magee?" asked Kate, just to make small talk.

"No, Kate. I am driving back to Ballyfauna later. I just drove down to meet Mary. Please call me David. Father is so formal."

"Ok, David," said Kate.

Bill was now standing next to David. "Tell me, Father, where were you before you came to us?"

"The Midlands," answered David. "Leitrim, to be precise."

Both men were about the same height and build, both handsome but in very different ways. Bill in an obvious way and David in a much more subtle way. David was, of course, older and greying and more mature looking. Kate could see why he might be attractive to a woman.

Bill suggested that they should go and have dinner. Kate knew that he meant the four of them, but Marcus asked David and Mary to join them. David thanked him for the kind invitation. "No thank you, Marcus. We had a big lunch, and I must be heading back and let my sister get back to her friends." He shook Marcus's hand warmly and thanked him again. She could see that the two men liked each other. David nodded to Bill. "Nice to meet you, Bill." Then he turned to Ciara and his sister, who had been chatting. "It is time for me to start for home, ladies."

They said goodbye to David and Mary. Ciara and Mary hugged as they parted, like they were old friends. Mary was a teacher at a small school in Cork, and the two of them had a lot in common. They promised to stay in touch. Ciara wished that she too was going home to process all the feelings that had come to the surface today. She really needed to be alone right now.

Bill was very quiet as they ate dinner. Kate was the only one who seemed to notice. Ciara and Marcus chatted away, but she was on autopilot.

"Seems like a nice man, your new boss, Ciara," Marcus said.

"Yes, he is, Marcus." Then she looked towards her husband. "What do you think now that you have met him, Bill?"

Without looking at her, he answered, "Same as any other priest, I suppose. You know I don't have much time for them."

Marcus's face registered surprise at the comment, but he said nothing.

As there were two more days before the first race day, Kate suggested that she and her sister should take time out for a bit of shopping and that perhaps the men would enjoy a few rounds of golf. It was clear that Kate had picked up on the tension between the younger couple and decided that some girl-time was needed.

Ciara wanted an early night and went to the room shortly after dinner. She got into bed, glad that Bill had stayed in the bar. Her mind was all over the place.

She still felt the shock of seeing David with a woman. She realised that this was what upset her most. But why? They just happened to run into her boss in the hotel bar. She introduced him and his sister to her family. That was all. Wasn't it? Why then couldn't she get him out of her head? If she wasn't careful Bill would definitely notice.

It had only been about two months since he walked into her office and she could never forget how she felt today seeing him with a woman.

Something had happened, and now she could no longer pretend to herself that he meant nothing to her. She had strong feelings for him and wanted him to stay. She wanted to talk to him, to listen to him and Marcus chat like old friends. She wished he was here now, beside her with his arms around her telling her that it would all be ok. But how could it be?

Chapter 9

She woke sometime later, to find that Bill had still not come to bed. She looked at her watch. It was 2.30am. He must have met with some people in the bar and stayed late. Either way she was glad that he wasn't there. By morning she might have some perspective and put her silly feelings aside. Everything would be ok. Yes everything would be okay, wouldn't it? Her thoughts lay unanswered.

Bill came into the room and a startled Ciara jumped up in the bed. "Bill, it's morning. Where on earth have you been?"

"Sorry if I gave you a fright. I had too much to drink last night and decided to walk it off. I'll have a shower now, and then we can go down for breakfast. Okay?"

"Yes, of course" was all she could muster. So, they were not going to discuss what was happening. That suited Ciara. There would be no more mention of Father David Magee for the rest of the week.

Their time was well planned, and they did everything in pairs or in a group. Everyone enjoyed the racing, and the weather was perfect. Tramore racecourse was less formal than The Curragh. The only time they were alone together was in bed, and while they were both polite to each other, no effort was made towards making love. It felt like they were treading on eggshells.

Early the next morning Bill had a phone call from a client, asking him to travel to Brussels with him for a few days during the week. He was buying into an Irish bar there and wanted Bill to go through the books. This was not unusual, and it seemed like a blessing at this time, for both of them. While the client was still on the phone, Bill looked at Ciara to see if she was ok with this and she nodded her agreement. He would be away until Thursday. This meant that they would miss the last day of racing. This new development was very welcome indeed. Ciara suspected that it suited everyone since they had not been the best of companions on this trip.

The following evening Ciara sat down to watch TV. She was much calmer now. Having had some time to herself, and a good chat with her sister today. They both agreed that Bill seemed to get over his thing about the PP. She didn't tell Kate that there was a distance between them in the bedroom.

Hopefully, by the time he got home, she would have worked out her feelings and be back to being the happily married woman that she was before. The sound of her phone disrupted her thoughts. She reached for it thinking that it would be her husband, checking in.

Instead, it was David. "Ciara, I hate to ask but…"

Chapter 10

"Not at all," she replied. "I will be there shortly." Her gut feeling was that she should not go to his house at this time of night, but she really wanted to see him, and as she told herself, he needed her help.

Ciara got in her car and drove to David's house. The door was already open for her. Stepping into the hall she called out, "David?"

He replied, "In here!" He stood up as she entered the small office just inside the door.

Moving passed him, she kept her eyes focussed on the computer. "Ok, let me see what the problem might be." He had been working on a sermon, and the document had gone off the screen. David was not good with technology. He was barely able to type.

When she sat down, she noticed that the leather seat was warm from him sitting there. Ciara began to check the screen and David crouched down beside her to see what she was doing. He was so close to her that she could feel the heat from his body and the sound of his breathing, very distracting. Though it unnerved her a little, she wanted him to stay there. She tried to concentrate on what she came here to do by talking him through what she was doing. She didn't dare turn to look at him. She knew that there was not much space between them. Finally, he stood up and asked if she would like a cup of tea. "Yes, please, that would be lovely."

As he walked out of the room, she turned in the chair and looked after him, and her heart did a summersault. Suddenly, Ciara knew that she had to get out of this house before she made a complete fool of herself. She wanted to reach out and touch him. This was a totally new sensation, one that threatened to overwhelm her. 'This has to stop,' Ciara said to herself. She grabbed her keys and bolted out the door without saying a word.

Back in the safety of her home, there was time to think. How the hell could she explain her actions?

When David came back with two cups of tea, he left one on the desk for her and began to drink the other thinking that she had gone to the bathroom. Eventually he went to check where his guest was, only to find that she had left. Shocked, David wondered, if she realised that he had gotten her there under false pretences? He would have to apologise, but how would he explain to her that he just wanted to see her, to be near her. What had he gotten himself into? What should he do? Ring her? Or leave her alone.

With that, the phone rang. It was Ciara.

"Sorry, I couldn't find your work," announced Ciara. "Then I remembered that I had left the oven on and left in a hurry." A lame excuse, but the only one she could come up with.

David wasn't sure what to make of this. Why hadn't she called out to him that she was leaving?

She continued to speak. "You must have deleted it. Perhaps you should leave the typing to me, Father? It is my job, after all. Just write it down and I will type it up for you." She was not sure whether he noticed how she addressed him.

The only word David did hear was 'Father'. Something was wrong. Had he said something to upset her? He shouldn't have asked her to come here.

"Ciara, could you have picked up my keys, by any chance? They were on my desk and now I can't find them."

"Hold on. I will have a look." It didn't take long to see that his keys were on the table inside her door.

"Yes, they are here Father. I am very sorry. I will return them immediately."

"Thank you, Ciara."

Time to calm down now, before going back to his house. After all, nothing had happened between them, and it was all in her mind.

Chapter 11

He had the door open again and this time he was waiting for her right inside the door. Ciara handed him the keys and made to leave, but David caught her hand gently. "Please come in." He led the way, not to the office, but to the living room. He asked her to sit down, and he did too. David was in charge now, and Ciara didn't dare to argue. She was too busy trying to keep her emotions in check.

"Have I upset you, Ciara?" he asked.

"No, not at all. Why do you say that?" she said looking at the floor.

"I noticed that you called me Father. You haven't done that since we met. Upsetting you is the last thing I want to do, Ciara. We work very well together, and I do enjoy your company."

'It is time to get out of here now,' thought Ciara. For a moment she imagined what it would be like to sit back in the chair and chat to him, tell him what she felt for him. He was talking now, but she was not listening.

Next thing she knew, David was standing in front of her. He had both hands extended. Without thinking, she put her hands in his and found herself moving towards him. They were face-to-face, no distance apart. She had no choice but to look him straight in the face.

"Ciara, are you ok?" he said, his voice full of tenderness and concern. All she could manage was a nod. "Is there something wrong? Talk to me, Ciara." What she saw on his handsome face was sadness and concern. In an instant, he drew her to his chest and wrapped both strong arms around her in a protective way, but with a single move the hug changed and became something else.

There was plenty of time to move back, create some distance and stop what was happening. Instead, Ciara looked up into his eyes. David looked different now. His concern was replaced by passion. He put his hand to her back and drew her forward until their bodies were as close as could be. Ciara raised her hands and wrapped them around his firm waist. As their lips met, so too did their bodies. Her hand moved up his back as she tried to move even closer to him. It was David who eventually pulled away.

"Are you sure about this, Ciara?"

Unable to speak, she put her hand to the back of his head and moved closer to kiss him again.

"I love you," he whispered. She could hear the passion in his voice. Neither one of them made any attempt to move away. Not another word was spoken. Ciara looked into his face. He kissed her again, gently at first, until their passion grew. It became a purely physical need and there was no turning back. They both started to remove each other's clothes until they were both naked from the waist up. The feel of his chest against her bare breasts was almost painful. He reached down to cup them. Ciara let out a moan. Her need for him was urgent. She wanted to be closer to him. She wanted him on top of her, inside her. She hoped he wouldn't stop. She lowered her hand to unzip his pants. That was when he scooped her up in his arms and carried her to his bed. She had never felt such passion with a man before. Any thoughts of Bill, long forgotten.

As they lay in each other's arms afterwards, Ciara ran her hand across his lean chest, half teasing him and half hoping that she could ignite his passion again. What happened next was even better than the first time. He called her name over and over. She felt one with him. They explored each other's bodies, giving and receiving all the pleasure they could. Ciara never knew that sex could be so beautiful and fulfilling. She loved him but couldn't remember if she had said it at the height of their passion. Neither of them spoke. It was almost as if talking would break the spell, and they both wanted to just lay there forever in each other's arms, their legs entwined, with no thought for the world outside. They were cocooned in their own private love.

As if reading her mind, David raised himself up on his elbow and looked down at her with sadness. He said, "Time to go home." She didn't want to go anywhere. Ciara looked at his chest and wanted to reach out and touch it. She wanted him to make love to her again and again.

He moved away from her. Her heart sank. He was getting out of bed and getting dressed.

"Are you sorry we did this, David?" she asked.

He answered without looking back. "I am only sorry that you have to go home to your husband." Those words cut through her like a knife.

Ciara started to get dressed, then remembered that some of her clothes were in the other room. She also remembered what an active part she had played in this – whatever should she call it? Well, whatever you'd call it, she knew that she would never regret it. David returned to the bedroom with the remainder of Ciara's clothing. He looked different. The spell had been broken. There were no words between them now. His expression told her that he didn't want to discuss it. She stayed quiet while she finished dressing. As she was about to leave, David put his arms around her the way you might if you were trying to protect someone. Then he looked down at her, his face full of emotion. "We will have to try to forget what happened between us tonight, Ciara. For your sake, for mine and for your husband's". As she was leaving, he kissed her tenderly and without the passion they shared earlier. It broke her heart to have to get in her car and drive away from him.

On the way home, Ciara knew one thing for sure. Her life had changed tonight and would never be the same again. How were they going to work together now? How was she going to live a life with Bill, have children, and forget what she felt for David, how it felt being in his bed, making love with him?

Chapter 12

Even in her present state, she recognised Bill's shiny black jeep outside the local pub. He wasn't due back until later in the week. Why didn't he ring and let her know that he was coming home early? That was the last thing she needed. In a moment of panic, she stopped the car and phoned Kate. "Can I come to you for the night, please?" was all she said. "If Bill rings, tell him that I am there with you, ok?"

"Of course. Drive carefully." Kate knew that something was very wrong with her sister.

The road to Naas over the Wicklow Mountains, while beautiful was also not to be undertaken without due care and attention, but it did give Ciara time to calm her thoughts of David and what had happened between them. She could still feel the pressure of his body on hers, how he smelled and how he said her name over and over. It was just three weeks since they had first met. But it could have been a lifetime. She felt like she had known and loved this man all her life.

What a mess, she thought as she drove into her sister's driveway.

"Any word from Bill?" said Ciara even before she greeted her sister.

"Yes, just now. I told him that you were asleep. Now what is going on? I thought he was away until later this week?" asked Kate.

Ciara started to cry. The tears rolled down her face uncontrollably. Kate got some tissues and let her cry it out, whatever it was. However, she was not prepared for what her sister had to tell her.

"Ciara! What were you thinking?" Kate was furious and not given to raising her voice, but this time was different. All professionalism went out the window. She was furious with her younger sister. "Of all the people you could have had an affair with, you had to pick the parish priest. Your boss, into the bargain! And what sort of man is he to allow this to happen? What a bloody mess you two have made!"

The sound of Kate's raised voice alerted Marcus in his study. "Okay, ladies, what is going on? Ciara, are you okay?"

Ciara wiped her eyes and said, "Yes Marcus, I am. Thank you."

"Good. That's all that matters then." Marcus was a typical surgeon and was not used to dealing with emotional matters. That was Kate's department. But this time she felt that he needed to know what was going on. This was not work, it was personal, and Kate felt out of her depth. She filled her husband in on the story. To diffuse a very tense situation, he asked if anyone would like some tea.

When he returned with a tray and three cups, he calmly said, "Well, it has happened now. You know that Kate and I are here for you, no matter what. What are you going to do, Ciara?" She began to cry again. Marcus was very good to her, and she didn't feel that she deserved any kindness at this time. "Let's start with a good night's sleep," he said. "we can chat more in the morning."

Ciara lay there in the bed that she had shared with her husband when they visited. But all she could think of was David. She felt numb. Was he ok? How was he feeling? Did he have any regrets about what they did? All these thoughts were swirling around her head.

Then she asked herself if this was a first for him, or had he had other affairs? Oh No, she felt stupid! With that, she jumped out of bed, trying to remember if he was an experienced man in bed. She began going over every bit of their lovemaking. She couldn't decide if he was or not. She had been so caught up in the moment and in what she was feeling, she hadn't been analysing him. She needed a drink of something stronger than tea.

It didn't take long before Kate was up too. "I'll join you in a glass of that," said Kate. Ciara told her sister of her fears about David. Kate laughed. It was a laugh of despair. "Little sister, think of what you have done, and you wonder if you are his first?" They hugged and laughed at the irony of it all.

The effect of the wine was beginning to kick in.

"Okay, the fact is you slept with a man, that isn't your husband. Bill doesn't need to know, if you don't want to tell him. Father Magee is not going to tell him. So, you two just have to live with it. You could get a new job if you don't want to work with him."

Just hearing her sister calling him Father made Ciara feel weird. When she was with him, he was just a man, not a priest. She had stopped thinking of him as a priest some weeks ago and allowed herself to have feelings for him.

"Some of this is my fault," announced Kate.

Ciara looked shocked "What? Why? What have you to do with it?"

"I could see it coming. I saw your face when he was on the phone to you at The Curragh and how you looked at each other in Tramore. I believe that Bill saw it too."

Chapter 13

Bill Parrish was not given to local gossip, but he decided that a trip to the local pub might be a good idea. He was filled with hatred for the parish priest. He had never seen his wife act the way she did when this man was around, and they were due back to work next Monday. He couldn't bear the thought of them being together at work, of that man being with her every day.

He knew he had to do something about it – and fast. He crafted a plan that would remove this man from their lives. Chuckling to himself, he knew that people loved to gossip. It would not be difficult to set in motion and he was happy to cast a little doubt over the oh so wonderful Fr Magee.

He was surprised to find the house was empty when he got home unexpectedly and immediately got suspicious. But after a phone call to Kate, he relaxed when he heard that she was with her sister. There was nothing more he could do now. Happy for the first time in a long time, Bill turned on the TV and watched it until he fell asleep.

Kate brought her sister some breakfast in the morning. They were both a bit the worse for wear from the night before, but Ciara was still an emotional mess. She just couldn't see a way out of it. Then to make things worse, Bill rang. He was in great form which made Ciara a little uneasy. Something was definitely up.

"Do you want me to join you there, darling?" he said.

Ciara could barely answer him. "No Bill, I am not feeling great. I will sleep on for a while and be home this evening."

"Yes, you do that. Love you, Ciara," he chirped and the phone went dead.

She told her sister about the call. "There you go. He realises that he has no reason to be jealous. Now all you have to do is forget about last night. It never happened, ok?" Ciara almost believed her sister, except for one thing. She wanted nothing more than to talk to David, to know that he was ok. When Kate left the room, she dialled his number. He answered immediately.

"Where are you?" he said, his voice full of emotion.

"I'm in Naas David. Are you alright?"

"Yes, no. Oh hell Ciara, I don't bloody know! Are you ok Ciara?"

"Yes," she said, "Bill just rang me. He is full of the joys of life. I don't know what that is about. He hasn't been like that for a while. Will we be able to get through this, David?"

"Yes, Ciara. We have no choice. I will see you back at work."

She didn't hear from him again during the week, even though she wanted to ring him every hour. She dared not do that. Bill continued with his upbeat mood. They carried on as if nothing was wrong, on the outside anyway. When they went to bed, Bill put a protective arm around his wife and Ciara was grateful that he didn't want to have sex with her. She couldn't bear that after having been with David. She didn't think that she could ever enjoy sex with another man again.

She was both looking forward to Monday and dreading it at the same time. However, everything changed on Friday night when she got a call from Ann O'Gorman, the school principal.

"Ciara, I have some very distressing news," said Ann.

"What is it, Ann?" said Ciara.

"It seems that there is a rumour going around about our parish priest."

Ciara's heart sank. She was barely able to talk. "What is it about, Ann?"

"They are saying that he was sent here after he was accused of child abuse in his last parish," said Ann. Ciara almost fainted.

After that conversation, she went and sat at the kitchen table and tried to process what she had just been told. This couldn't be true. It just couldn't.

It could have been fifteen minutes or fifteen hours, Ciara didn't know how long she had been there at the table, but when she came to her senses, she knew that she had to phone him. The phone rang for a while before he answered.

"Ciara, we can't talk," he said.

"We have to, David. There is a rumour going around about you," Ciara said.

"I know."

"What are you going to do?"

"Are you going to ask if it is true, Ciara?"

"No, I am not!" she exclaimed.

There was silence. "Thank you. That's all I need to know."

Tears flowed down her face, and she wished she could put her arms around him. She knew for sure then that she loved this man and would do anything in the world to help him.

"I have to inform the Bishop," David said. "I don't know when I will see you. I will ring you if at all possible, Ciara." That was when she wanted to say, 'I love you, David,' but she didn't. The phone went dead.

Chapter 14

Ciara said nothing to Bill about what was happening. She felt sure that he would gloat, and she couldn't bear that. He got home early and tried to cajole her to go into town for dinner, but she pretended to have a headache and went to bed. Bill went to the local for a drink.

Having cried herself to sleep, she woke from time to time thinking that she was having a nightmare, only to realise that this was really happening. She had no choice but to wait and see what happened next. She was only half asleep when Bill got home. She could hear him whistling in the kitchen – that was not like him at all. He made sure that she heard him as he came into the bedroom.

"Hi darling, you'll never guess what I heard in the pub." He was drunk. "Wake up Ciara! You'll want to hear this. Your friend David is a paedophile. Do you hear me?"

Ciara sat up in bed and looked at him. "What are you talking about, Bill? Where did you hear such a thing?"

"In the pub. Everyone is talking about it. Some people are not sending their children back to school if he is still there." He stumbled and landed on the bed.

Ciara jumped out of the bed as if she had been attacked. "You are drunk!" she shouted at her husband for the first time since they had met. "And what's more, you are fucking stupid if you believe what you hear from gossip in the pub. Someone had nothing better to do than to start that rumour, and you, an educated man, come in here, repeating it as if it were gospel. Well, I don't believe it. I am going to sleep in another room."

She didn't go to bed, what was the point? It wasn't as if she could sleep. She had a few glasses of wine and was a bit groggy when the phone rang. She was just about able to see the time on the big kitchen clock. It was ten past nine. She picked up the receiver hoping that it was David. Instead, a man with a stern voice greeted her.

"Mrs Parrish?"

"Yes, speaking," said Ciara.

"My name is Father O'Donnell. I work in the Bishop's office. Father Magee has had to go away on private business for a while. A replacement will be provided for Saturday and Sunday Mass. If you have any issues in the office you can ring Father Magee's number, and we will be here for you. Do you have any questions, Mrs Parrish?" he said.

"No, Father. Thank you."

That was it.

Ciara always had friends, but none like her sister. She would have to ring Kate and Marcus but first she would have to pull herself together. After a shower, she tried to eat some breakfast, but couldn't. She phoned Ann and filled her in. Ann was non-committal on the issue and asked about the practical stuff such as who would say mass, was there a new priest coming? Her attitude didn't help at all. It sounded like David had been found guilty.

Chapter 15

It wasn't long before Marcus and Kate arrived. They both looked like Ciara felt and as bad as that was, it helped to know that they didn't believe the story. Kate looked around as she plugged in the kettle.

"Where is Bill? Gone to the office?"

"No, Bill is in bed. He came home late last night very drunk. He woke me up to tell me the news."

"Oh," said Kate. "He is not much help then."

"No. Well, you know how he feels about Father David. This is right up his alley. He is rid of him, or so he thinks. But I am not giving up on him. I will get to the bottom of this," said Ciara.

"Can this be a coincidence? Did anyone see you at the parochial house, Ciara?

Kate put her arms around her sister, and the tears flowed like never before.

Marcus came over to them. "It's ok, Ciara. We will sort this out. It's just not right, and we have to fight it. A man can't be condemned for such a crime based on gossip from Ballyfauna." Marcus, practical as ever, sat down and reached for pen and paper. "Now Ciara, do you know where David was before he came here?" A simple question, but it told her that she knew nothing about this man. All she knew was that she loved him.

It was ten-thirty before Bill arrived down for breakfast. He was surprised to find his in-laws in the kitchen, and his wife distressed. He stood there, with a look of surprise on his face. "What's wrong?"

Marcus stood up and told him that Father Magee had been removed from the parish because of a rumour of child sex abuse going around Ballyfauna. "We have to do something to help the man, Bill," said Marcus calmly. "This is just not right."

Bill went to the coffee maker and poured himself a cup. He went to sit by his wife and put his arm around her. "Are you ok? Look, I know you like the man but who knows, maybe he's not as innocent as he appears?"

Ciara jumped up. "Well, you never liked him from the start, even before you met him!"

Bill stood up and faced her. "Well, you think he hung the moon!"

Kate stood up and shouted. "Stop it, you two! You are not helping."

"Ok, let's sit down and see what we can do to help the poor man," said Marcus.

Bill sat down. He didn't look like his heart was in it, but he didn't want to go against Marcus. Marcus was the one person that he looked up to, and this was not worth falling out over. The priest was gone, and now things could go back to normal.

Marcus was wise enough not to ask Ciara what she knew about Father Magee. Instead he went in another direction. "Let's turn on the computer and find out what parishes he served in."

Then Ciara jumped in. "Let's talk to his sister."

Bill excused himself from the group, saying that he had to go into the office. He kissed Ciara on the forehead, said goodbye to Kate and Marcus and left. Ciara reached for her phone and searched for Mary's number.

Kate jumped up to grab Ciara's phone. "No. Don't do that. You can't just tell the girl that her brother is involved in a scandal like this. Not until we know more, at least."

Marcus took charge of the situation. "Ciara, your laptop please, and some coffee, if you wouldn't mind?" He looked up the diocese for County Leitrim where Father David Magee had come from. Marcus had lots of contacts around the country. It was time for some detective work. The sisters left that to Marcus. He made notes and then at least three phone calls. He spoke to people whom he trusted to ask such questions of and came up with nothing to suggest that there had ever been any question about Father David Magee in the past.

This was a great help to Ciara.

Marcus and Kate had to go home to Naas as they both had work commitments later that day. After they had gone, Ciara felt alone. She knew that Bill could not help her in this situation. Ciara also knew that David's phone was in the hands of the church, and there was no way to contact him. She would just have to wait for him to ring her. There was less than a week before the school opened again. That would barely give her time to come to terms with recent events. Bill kept his distance since the news broke. They were never going to be able to talk about this without being on opposite sides.

At the local shop, people she knew all wanted to know what she thought of the latest news. As Ciara was the only who had worked with this new parish priest since he arrived, everyone wanted to know what she thought about it. Where is he now and why did he run away, they asked. She also heard the whispers. "There is no smoke without fire!" they said. When asked directly, Ciara gave them her honest view. "I have worked with Father Magee for the past month. He is a nice decent man. I believe that this is a vicious rumour without any sort of proof whatsoever and the gossip needs to end." Joan the shopkeeper, nodded in agreement, but Ciara doubted that she was going to do anything to stop the spread of this juicy story. They didn't know this man and didn't care if they destroyed his character.

She kept calm and left the shop but as soon as she got into her car, the tears began. It was difficult to drive home. Ciara parked in front of Ivy Manor and just sat in the car and cried until she could cry no more. She would have to find him, somehow.

Kate would not let her ring Mary Magee, but Mary was the only link she had, and she was going to take the chance and call her. Ciara had the number saved in her phone but paused before she hit the button. All sorts of scenario flew through her mind, then she did it. Mary answered immediately.

"Oh, thank God you rang Ciara," Mary was obviously distressed. "We need to meet up, if that's ok with you?" They arranged to meet that day and Ciara said nothing to anyone about it. David had rung his sister, but the details were very sketchy.

Chapter 16

When they met, the two women hugged like old friends and Mary was glad that she had contact with at least one person from Ballyfauna who knew her brother, and hopefully believed that he was innocent.

"Do you know where he is?" Ciara gushed. "Is he ok?"

"I have no idea," said Mary. "I thought you might know."

Ciara told Mary what she knew of the situation. Mary started to cry. "This is awful, Ciara. How am I going to help him? I don't believe the church is going to do much for him. They just want to cover their own backs. They would not even tell us where he is, and they have his phone. Where did this accusation come from, Ciara? Do you know?"

"I'm sorry, Mary. I have no idea, but we will get to the bottom of it. I promise you. Do you have any idea where he might go to, Mary? Other family members, friends? When did he ring you? Was it before he told the bishop?"

"Yes, Ciara, he told me that there was a rumour doing the rounds about him and he had to inform the Bishop and that he would ring me later."

"I suppose we will have to talk to the bishop, Mary. Perhaps if you ask, they might tell you where he is, or at least give you a phone number for him."

The two women left the restaurant where they were and went to sit in Mary's car. Ciara had the phone number on her phone, and she called it out to Mary. They waited and listened as the phone was answered.

"Hello, my name is Mary Magee. I am the sister of Father David Magee. Can you tell me where I can find him please?"

"Father O'Donnell here," said a rather stern voice. "I am sorry Ms Magee, your brother is on sabbatical at the moment and cannot be reached at this time. Can I give him a message for you?"

"No, thank you," said Mary. "Could you please give me his phone number?"

"I am sorry, Ms Magee. You have no need to worry. Your brother will be in touch when the time is right for him to do so. Goodbye."

The line went dead.

Mary cried for her brother, but Ciara had to hold back her tears even though her heart was breaking. Mary looked to Ciara. "What am I going to do? Do I tell my parents?"

"No. Don't tell anyone, this would break your parent's hearts. We have no choice but to wait and hope he will be in touch."

The two women said goodbye, promising to stay in touch as they went in opposite directions.

Ciara went home to an empty house. She made a light lunch for herself but couldn't eat it. She went to bed instead. When she closed her eyes and imagined David lying there beside her, his lovely smiling face close to hers as she remembered his passionate kisses and their bodies close together. That was all she had now. The memories seemed like such a long time ago, so much had happened since that beautiful night. What a mess, she thought, as the tears streamed down her face.

She must have slept for a long time, for the next thing she heard was Bill coming into the room and sitting on the bed beside her. She pretended to be asleep, but he shook her, and she had no choice but to open her eyes and look up at him. He leaned down and kissed her on the cheek. Ciara wanted to pull away from him. How was she going to deal with this?

Bill went downstairs to make them dinner. He was happy now that he had his wife's full attention again. She had no choice but to go down and eat with her husband, no matter how difficult that might be. The table was set, and the smell of fresh salmon was delicious, there was a bottle of white wine on ice. He was going all out to impress her.

She wondered if he had any idea how she was feeling or the devastation that was going on in her mind. He looked like a stranger to her, a man she barely knew. He pulled out her chair and she sat down. Before they would both have laughed about this and she would have felt very fortunate to have such a good husband, but now she just had to eat her food and look like she was enjoying it. Bill talked during the meal and Ciara had no idea what he was saying, they were just words about his work.

As they finished, the phone rang, it was Kate. She put the speaker on, and Marcus was there with her. Kate asked how they were, then went on to tell them that Marcus had been in touch with friends who lived in Leitrim where Father Magee had been for the past four years. There were never any accusations against him there, and no one had ever heard anything from his past. Marcus's friends were shocked and upset at this new development.

"We need to get in touch with him," said Marcus. "Ciara, do you have a phone number for him?"

"No Marcus, the bishop's office has his phone, and his sister has no idea where he is."

There was silence.

"I thought we agreed to wait until we did some research before we got in contact with her," said Kate.

"Oh, I forgot," lied Ciara.

"Has he told his sister what has happened?" asked Marcus.

"Yes," said Ciara, "but not his parents."

"Hopefully, they will never have to hear such news about their son," said Kate.

Bill didn't say a word. He just sat there looking disinterested.

"Ok," said Marcus, "there is not much more we can do until we hear from David, but I think we can safely say that the rumour is false and the people who started it have a lot to answer for."

They said goodbye and hung up.

Ciara looked at Bill and asked what he thought about the phone call. His answer didn't really surprise her.

"Well, I don't know why they are bothered about him. It's not as if they really knew him, is it?" he said.

"No, but they did like him when they met in Tramore. They are trying to help me realise that I was not wrong about Father Magee. Surely I would have picked up something in the time we worked together in the last few weeks." She was angry with her husband and wanted to add 'and the night we slept together', but she kept her mouth shut.

The phone call had helped Ciara realise that she was not alone. Sadly, it made her feel very lonely in her own home.

What now? Would she just wait and hope that David Magee was feeling the same way as her? How the hell could she live with Bill now that she was in love with another man? What was going to happen to the life that she had planned with Bill, the children that were going to grow up in Ivy Manor?

Chapter 17

I t was Monday, and the school was reopening. Ciara went into the office, but her heart was not in it. She was on autopilot. Just as she had expected, the teachers all wanted to know what was happening and if Father Magee was coming back. Ciara gave the same answer to everyone. "I have no idea." then turned back to her desk and pretended to be busy. She did not want to answer the endless questions about what sort of man he was. They had seen him say Mass on three occasions, and none of them had met him, but they all knew that she had been working with him for several weeks and she must know more.

Halfway through the morning, the phone rang. As she answered she knew immediately that it was not David. It was Father O'Donnell from head office.

"Hello Mrs Parrish. I hope all is well in Ballyfauna," he said.

"Yes, Father. It is." Ciara didn't feel like being polite to this man, who was holding David's phone and keeping her from talking to him.

"That's good. Just ring if you need anything," he replied.

Then she remembered her calls to and from David and wondered if the bishop's office had looked through the call log and seen how many calls they had made to each other. He informed her that he was putting a priest in place for Mass at the weekend and that she should continue to support him as she had with other priests before him. "Yes Father," was all she could bring herself to say. "Goodbye."

Putting the phone down, she was livid. This bloody man and the bishop have listened to gossip and sent David away. They have his phone, and now he spoke as if he had never been there. How can this be right? Surely they should be standing up for him, supporting him and his family. He gave up his life to the church when he could have had a proper family. One that gathers around him in his time of need. Ciara was not giving up on him – not now, not ever – and she knew that she was not alone. She had Mary, Marcus and Kate, and they would get to the bottom of this.

When lunchtime came, Ciara didn't want to sit with the teachers as she usually did. She got into her car and went home. She was surprised to find Bill there. He regularly ate in town at this time of day. He was upbeat in his manner and didn't notice that his wife was subdued. As she put a salad together, he came up behind her, put his arms around her and kissed the back of her neck. Ciara cringed and wanted to get away from him, but she had no place to go.

Not long ago, in this situation, she would get turned on by the heat from his body and they would have had sex, there and then, in the kitchen. Ciara would go back to work smiling. Now she turned around and slapped her husband in the face. "Get away from me," she shouted. It worked. Bill stepped back in shock. He looked like he had seen a ghost.

"What the hell is wrong with you, Ciara?" he said in a shocked voice.

He clearly had no idea what was going on in her head and in her heart. 'What the fuck is wrong with him?' she thought. She had lost her appetite and went to the bathroom to try and calm herself. That didn't work because all she wanted to do was cry, and she had to go back to work. Her phone rang, it was Kate checking to see how she was doing. "Not good, sis. I just want to run away and be on my own, far away from Bill. I hate being in the house with him, being anywhere near him."

"Okay, come and stay here for a while. You can't work in this condition. Ring in sick. Let the bishop replace you."

With that, Ciara laughed. "You are right! He is very bloody good at replacing people. Thanks, Kate. I'll see you later. You are a lifesaver."

After Bill left the house, Ciara made a phone call to the bishop's office to say that she was unwell and was taking some time off. She then packed a suitcase, not just an overnight bag. It was big enough for someone not planning to return anytime soon. Then she wrote a short note to Bill telling him of her plan, but only a short version. As she sat into the car and looked up at the house, she had the distinct feeling that she would not live the rest of her life in Ivy Manor, nor would they have the children that Bill longed for. She left the house and drove towards Naas over the Wicklow mountains.

After driving about ten kilometres she stopped. It was time to think about the mess she was running away from. What had happened to her dream life? It was just two weeks since the night when she and David could not deny the passion between them. It seemed like a lifetime ago. She knew that her life had changed but had no idea how much. Bill would never be the same to her and their life together now looked fake. It was like watching a romantic movie. It was as if they had never been in love at all, not real love. Then she thought of the weeks working with David, the feelings she had when they sat together in the office and when he phoned her. How they had made love. The tears came rolling down her cheeks. She ached to put her arms around him, just one more time – if that's all she could have. She cried for a long time until she was so tired that she wanted to close her eyes there and then and sleep. Not a good idea. It would be getting dark and not safe for a woman on her own to sleep in a car. Anyway, Kate would be expecting her.

Chapter 18

Kate only had to take one look at her sister to know that she had been crying and there was no need to ask why. With her arms still around her sister, Kate asked, "Any word from David?"

Ciara noticed that she didn't call him Father. "I wish I knew where he is and that he is ok. I will ring Mary after we have a cup of tea to see if she knows anything."

"Ok, put your case in the bedroom and I will put the kettle on," said Kate.

Mary was glad to hear from Ciara. At least someone else was concerned for her brother.

"No Ciara, not a word. I am worried, not only for his physical safety but his mental state."

Ciara could not tell Mary about her feelings for her brother, as they may not be reciprocated. "Try not to worry too much, Mary. He will ring you when the time is right. Can you think of any friends who he might have gone to stay with?" Ciara asked.

"No, most of his friends would be from around this part of Cork, and I can't ask anyone for obvious reasons." Then she added that she had phoned the bishop's office in Wicklow and they told her that Father Magee was on sabbatical and would be assigned a new parish in due course. "Thank God for you, Ciara. You are the only person in the world that I can talk to about this. He is my brother, and they speak of him as if he belongs to them, their property. This can't be right, none of it. I know that David never interfered with children or anyone else, and it looks to me as if the church doesn't believe him. That's what hurts the most, Ciara."

"I know what you mean. If there was only some way that we could find out where it all started…"

When Ciara finished talking to Mary Magee, she looked at Kate with wide eyes. "They have removed him from Ballyfauna. No investigation, no attempt to find out who started the story – nothing! This is crazy. It's just not good enough!" She was glued to a spot on the floor. "A man comes to our parish, has his reputation destroyed and the church does nothing to help him."

Kate put a drink into her sister's hand. "Here. Sit down and drink that." All of Kate's training had not prepared her for this. Dealing with patients was different from watching your sister going through what looks like a breakdown and not knowing what to say to make her feel better. Kate also knew that it was only a matter of time until Bill turned up, asking questions. How the hell was she going to deal with him? She could hardly tell him the truth, nor could she lie to him.

Kate sat down beside Ciara and put a throw over their knees. "Don't worry, sis, we will sort this out."

Suddenly, Ciara sat bolt upright in the chair. "Who would have a grudge against David in Ballyfauna?" Bill was the first name that came to her.

"Now," said Kate, "Bill wouldn't do such a thing. It would have to be someone with a very twisted mind and that is not your husband."

Later that night after Ciara had gone to bed, Kate told Marcus about their conversation.

"No," said Marcus, "that is not Bill's style. Anyway, why would he?"

Kate decided to tell Marcus the full story. She started with her initial suspicions and with Bill's jealousy. She told him her own observations since The Curragh up until the night Ciara and David slept together. Marcus was speechless. Kate put her arms around him. "Sorry hun, it's true."

Marcus moved away abruptly, with a shocked look on his face. He said, "So Ciara is here in bed. Bill is at home. David is God knows where?" He was not given to swearing, but this was different. "For fuck sake!" he shouted. "What is going on?"

It was Kate's turn to pour two glasses of wine.

"Ciara is prepared to believe that Bill started the rumour about David. What do you think, hun?"

Marcus sat back on the sofa, clutching his wine glass and trying to get his head around this crazy situation. "To be honest, Kate, I don't know who or what to believe. And there are no winners in this mess. I'm free tomorrow and will call down to Bill and see what he really knows. Then again, perhaps we should wait for him to come here. I think it best to let them think about it and sort it out themselves. They are adults, after all." At that same point, Marcus and Kate looked at each other and rolled their eyes.

As the days passed without a word or a call from Bill, Marcus and Kate carried on with their daily lives and went to work. As far as they could tell, Ciara didn't leave the house. Most days she didn't even get dressed.

Ciara spent her days hoping for a call from David Magee. Why didn't he ring her? He must have a new phone by now, and it wouldn't be difficult to find her number. Perhaps he did this all the time. Maybe she should try to forget him.

She was in Naas four days before she got a letter in the post.

Chapter 19

Dearest Ciara,

I am trying to give you as much time as you need to sort out your feelings.

You need to know that I love you and always will. I want nothing more than to have you back here with me, where you belong. Don't worry about your job, you don't need to work. Why don't you and I take a luxury holiday in the sun and get back to where we were before?

Love

Bill XX

She read and reread it. Not sure what to make of it. It seemed simple to him. Go on a luxury holiday, give up my job and be a good wife. Simple as that. She felt a bit sorry for her husband just then. He had no idea that his wife had been unfaithful and was in love with another man, but he would have to be told. She could not let him go on thinking that they would ever get back to normal. Even if she never saw David again, she no longer loved Bill Parrish. Now she was crying not just for David and herself but for Bill and the life they had been building together at Ivy Manor. If there was one good thing about this entire mess, it was that there were no children involved.

She showed Kate the letter that evening. With her psychologist hat on, Kate reflected before making a comment. She turned from where Ciara was sitting at the breakfast bar, where she spent a lot of her time these last few days, drinking tea and wine.

"Perhaps you should go on a holiday. Give yourself time to relax with Bill, away from normality and Ballyfauna and all reminders of Father David Magee." Kate came around to where her sister was sitting and put a protective arm around her. "Ciara, if your marriage is over, you need to make sure of that before you tell Bill what happened. I don't believe that he is one to forgive and forget after you tell him."

"Ok," said Ciara. "I will think about what you said."

Four days later Ciara drove back to Ballyfauna. She had no idea what she was going to say to Bill. He was still at work when she got home. She decided to call to see the parish priest and tell him that she would not be coming back to work. One thing that she was sure about was that she would not work for the Catholic church again, and she said as much to him, without mentioning David's name. He told her that he was very sorry to hear that, as she was well suited to the job and, by all accounts, very good at it.

She then went to her office and collected a few personal things that she had there. She noticed that the two chairs were still in place, where she and David had worked together. She had a lump in her throat but smiled and said goodbye to Ann and the other teachers. Just saying that she was going to a new job, being careful not to give them any reason for her decision. They were not to know that Ciara had no idea where her life was going from here.

Bill was there when she returned home. He came towards her with his arms open wide. She accepted his embrace. "I am delighted to have you back, darling."

Ciara wasn't feeling any romance, there was no spark, no excitement. All the feelings that used to be there were gone. She moved away from him and made herself busy in the kitchen.

Bill didn't give up. "How about a cruise?" he said.

"Yes. That sounds nice. When do we go?"

"The day after tomorrow. I just booked it today," he said.

'Oh, you were very sure of yourself,' thought Ciara. "Ok, I had better start packing then."

"Just pack a few things. You can do some shopping as we go." Bill really had thought about this and was spending a lot of money in his bid to win her back.

In her gut, she knew that it was a waste of money, but she had to give it a try, and since her husband was tight with money generally, Ciara wasn't feeling too guilty. On their bed, she saw the details of the European cruise. They were to fly to Barcelona and the cruise would take them to visit Naples, Rome, Florence, Cannes and Palma.

Their cabin had a balcony and butler service. Under normal circumstances, she would be over the moon, but she felt none of the excitement that would come with such a trip. However, they were going, and she had better start packing.

Bill came into the room as she was putting clothes into a case. He picked up their itinerary and asked, "What do you think? Are you excited?"

"Yes, it looks great." He was happy with that.

Ciara made dinner. The conversation between them was strained. They both steered away from why she had felt the need to go to Naas for a few days. She told him that she had given notice at her job. This brought a smile to Bill's face, and Ciara wanted to slap him. He didn't ask why she had done this. 'He probably thinks that I am going to work for him. Not a chance,' thought Ciara, 'not in a million years.'

Later that night, she realised that she was going to have to sleep with her husband. She had better get her mind straightened out.

She had slept with David Magee, days later he left and had not been in touch with her since. If he had felt any of what she was feeling, he would have found a way to contact her. He hadn't. Now she would have to get over him. Perhaps she could fall back in love with Bill on the cruise. She made sure that she was in bed first, settled in and with her back to him. She hoped that when Bill did come to bed, he would not disturb her or try to make love to her.

With just one day to get ready to go on the cruise. Ciara decided to go into town and have her hair and nails done. Bill had a busy day making sure that the office would run without him and that Johnny would be around to check on the house. While at the hairdressers Ciara got a call from Mary Magee. Mary was upbeat, and Ciara knew straight away that she had heard from David. She held her breath and waited to see what Mary was going to say.

"He's ok, Ciara," said Mary. "He is staying with another priest in London, waiting to be told of his future."

Ciara excused herself and left the hairdresser standing there stunned, as she walked to the door of the salon with water dripping off her hair. "So, is he going to defend himself against this allegation, Mary? Surely it can't just be left like this, with him branded a paedophile."

"I don't know, Ciara I told him that you and your family were of great support to me and he is very grateful to you for that."

She desperately wanted to ask for his phone number but couldn't do that. Mary may suspect something, and she and her family had enough to worry about without knowing that he had slept with a married woman. Contact would have to come from him.

"I am glad that he's ok and got in touch with you, Mary. Feel free to give him my phone number, should he wish to talk to me," Ciara said.

"Ok, thanks, Ciara. I will keep that in mind."

Chapter 20

As they boarded the cruise ship, a woman smiled at them and Ciara could imagine what the woman must be thinking; a very stylish couple off to enjoy themselves and all that the cruise ship had to offer. If she only knew that the woman would prefer to be anywhere but here with the handsome dark-haired man in the well-fitted check shirt and white pants and, of course, designer deck shoes. Bill was excited, and Ciara was still amazed that he had spent a fortune on this trip. It was very extravagant, and he was not that sort of man. He was clearly desperate to win her back.

When they got to their cabin, it was beautiful. What a view and it had a hot tub on the balcony. The furniture was modern and luxurious. It was everything you could ask for and more. She couldn't help but smile at Bill as they looked around the ship in amazement.

"Thank you," she said and went to kiss him on the cheek.

Bill put his arms around her for the first time in a long time. He looked down at her. "Let's just enjoy this, Ciara."

She smiled back and nodded. "Yes, let's do that."

There was that much to see on board that no matter what circumstances brought you here, you could not ignore the beauty of this ship. There were two luxury bathrobes and slippers laid out on the bed. Bill started to unpack their bags.

"Where would you like your things?" he said.

"I'm not fussy," answered Ciara as she slid open the balcony door and stepped out. She felt excited for the first time and wished her sister was here to see this first-hand. She doubted she could describe it and do it justice.

When he finished putting their clothes in the right place, Bill suggested that they go and have a look around.

They stepped out of the lift and straight into a shopping mall. It was bright and colourful, with designer goods everywhere. Bill caught her hand, squeezed it and leaned down and said in a low voice, "Remember now, Ciara, this is a one-off trip. Buy what you want. I want to spoil you."

She looked up at him, and he kissed her cheek, tenderly. "Ok," said Ciara, "let's shop!" and she laughed out loud. They both looked at the costly things and shook their heads, laughing. They tried stuff on and discussed whether it suited them. They were smiling at each other and having fun, and it felt good.

"Ok, enough shopping for today," said Bill and he took their purchases back to the cabin while Ciara sat in a comfortable chair and waited. It wasn't long before she was thinking of David, she could not imagine him here. Bill broke into her thoughts. "Ok, Mrs Parrish, where to now?"

The day passed quickly as they explored the ship, and they ended with a beautiful dinner and two bottles of the best wine. They chatted easily about the experience and what else they would do while on-board and day trips they would like to take. As they finished the second bottle of wine, it was clearly time to call it a day. When they got into bed, Bill put his hand across Ciara's waist, he looked at her lovingly and said, "I hope you had a good day, darling."

Ciara smiled back at him and said, "Yes Bill, it was fantastic and it's only the first day."

He kissed her on the forehead and turned over.

Ciara was shocked but glad that he had not wanted to have sex tonight. She was resigned to the fact that they would on this trip, and hopefully, she would be ready when the time came. If their physical relationship could not be restored, then it would be over. She was lying in the same direction as Bill and looking at his straight back and broad shoulders as she thought, 'What woman would not want to have this man in her bed?' Then once again, David Magee crept into her mind, and she turned over and couldn't help but remember that night and wished with all her heart that he was here in her bed.

Thinking about him made her feel stupid. He was gone to England and had a new phone number. There was nothing to stop him from ringing her, but he didn't. He had turned her life upside down and just walked away. At that moment, Ciara felt that her heart would break. Her tears flowed into her pillow. Thank God her husband was sleeping peacefully, totally unaware of the turmoil that was going on in her heart.

The cruise was terrific. Their days were full of new things and new places to visit. They bought presents for family and friends. They laughed and chatted as they did so. Bill put his arm around her from time to time and she didn't resist. She could see that he was delighted with this, and while it didn't feel as natural as it used to, there was no point in not trying to repair their relationship.

The Captain's Party is a big deal, formal wear a must. Bill had his tuxedo in the wardrobe, but he wanted to treat Ciara to a new dress for the occasion. After a light lunch on the deck, he caught Ciara's hand. "Come on, Mrs Parrish. Let's find you a knock-out dress!"

She wished that he would stop reminding her that she was his wife. Heading into the first shop in the mall, Bill pulled her back. "No not there. Let's go to one of the better shops.

Ciara giggled. "What has happened to the accountant in you, Bill?"

He took both her shoulders and looked into her face. "I want everything about this holiday to be unique, and that includes your dress for tonight." He kissed her on the lips this time and held her hand as they approached the most expensive shop on the ship. With the help of two assistants, she stood in the most amazing pink dress. She felt like a film star. One of the ladies pulled her hair up to show her how it could look. Ciara was impressed. She walked out to let Bill see it. He was not as excited about it as she was.

"Ok, next," he said.

Ciara was taken aback. "You don't like this one?"

"Well yes, but you could try a few. It's not every day that you get to buy a dress like this."

"I suppose you're right." She tried on two more before she came out in a red halter neck that fitted like a glove.

Bill's face lit up. "Whoa!" he said, "Now that's more like it. All you need a necklace to go with it. Let's hit the jewellers."

She grabbed his hand. "No Bill, I have a chain in the cabin." But he insisted that she have a new one. Finally, she gave in. "But let's get one from here. We don't have to pay a fortune for it." Once again, the shop assistants got busy and took pieces out of glass cabinets. Ciara liked a plain gold one. She looked at her husband for approval as he was paying for it and once again, he didn't approve. Instead, he reached into the cabinet and took out an exquisite one made up of coloured stones, set in gold. Not the real thing but expensive, neverthe-less. Yes, it would complement the dress, and yes, Bill had great taste in all things.

When they got back to their cabin, it was a beau-tiful sunny evening. She poured two glasses of cham-pagne and walked out onto their balcony, where her husband was sitting. "Imagine if Kate and Marcus were here to enjoy this," she said, looking out at the horizon. Bill took the glass from her and smiled. "I am happy that it's just us. I love spending time with my beautiful wife away from the rest of the world." He raised his glass. "To us," he said, and Ciara raised her glass.

It was time to shower for the formal night out, and part of Ciara was excited at the prospect. She was in her robe going towards the bathroom when Bill put his hand on her shoulder and came around in front of her, he looked down and gently opened the robe putting his hands inside it and around her slim waist, then very slowly he lifted her chin and kissed her. Ciara knew that this was coming and decided not to put it off any longer. As his kiss became more passionate, she responded but not to him, in her mind it was David she was going to have sex with. To Bill's delight, she returned his kiss with equal passion. There was a hunger in them both. They made love like never before. Afterwards, she lay in his arms, closed her eyes and pretended that he was David Magee.

Bill was apparently happy that everything was working the way he had planned. He had finally got his wife back, and he could not be any happier. When Ciara appeared in the red dress with her hair in an up style, she took his breath away. He too was ready and looking dashing as usual. As she put on her earrings, he came and stood slightly to the left of her, in front of the mirror. They certainly did look good together, and yes, the red was beautiful but not her choice. Ciara would have felt better in the pale pink, it was less obvious. She preferred to blend in, not stand out, however, there was no blending in tonight. He kissed the nape of her neck and whispered, "I am extremely glad that we are back on track, sweetheart. I couldn't live without you, Ciara." His words sent a chill through her, and she wished that she felt the same. No more time for reflection, Bill took her hand and led her to the lift that brought them to the main event.

As expected, heads turned as they entered the room and Bill liked it. They were led to their places at the large round table. Ciara was seated beside a nice homely lady from Yorkshire, and they hit it off immediately. They talked about the food, the cruise, and life in general. The woman's name was Sally. She and her husband were celebrating thirty years of marriage. She leaned close and whispered, "Most of it happy!" and they laughed like old friends.

Leaning towards Bill, Ciara commented on the food, but he didn't hear her. He was engrossed in conversation with the man seated on the other side of him. Later in the night, they danced, and she could tell how proud he was of his beautiful wife and how well they danced together. When they sat down, Sally said, "What a beautiful couple you make! Right out of Hollywood." Bill would be delighted with that comment, but she wasn't going to tell him.

Ciara and Sally arranged to meet the next day, without their husbands, for coffee. Time away from Bill seemed like a luxury at this stage. It was their second last port visit and much as she would like to visit Corfu, time out was more important right now. However, she persuaded Bill to go alone while she met Sally. Sally was pleasant and had a good sense of humour, just what the doctor ordered. Ciara missed her sister, but they had made a deal that Ciara would spend her time with Bill and try to get back what they had lost. It was Kate's idea – the psychologist coming out in her, but now it was time for some female company. Bill held her tight and kissed her before he left, clearly disappointed that she was not coming with him.

Chapter 21

The two women met at the appointed time in the coffee shop and ordered two cappuccinos. As Ciara lifted the coffee to take a sip, she was overcome by the smell of it and quickly put it down again. Sally noticed and asked if the coffee was ok.

"It just doesn't smell right," said Ciara. "How is yours?"

"Very good," replied Sally. Ciara picked up her coffee, and as she put it to her mouth, she felt herself heave and almost get sick. She excused herself and went to the bathroom. She had a drink of water, washed her hands and went back to Sally.

"Are you ok?" asked Sally.

"Yes, thank you." She called the waiter and ordered a fresh orange juice.

Sally was in her mid-forties and had two children, old enough to be left alone now. She asked Ciara if she was planning to have children.

"Yes," answered Ciara, "I would like to have at least two when the time is right."

Sally caught her hand and said, "Babies will come even if you think the time is not perfect." Still holding her hand, Sally faced Ciara. "Is now a good time for you to have a baby?"

"No," said Ciara, "Bill and I have a few issues, but hopefully, we will get over them and have our family."

Sally laughed. "Ciara?"

"Yes, Sally?"

There was a long pause.

The older woman took both of Ciara's hands now. "Could you be pregnant now?"

Ciara laughed. "No, I could not. Unless it happened yesterday!"

Sally let go of Ciara's hands, and the subject was not mentioned again as they sat in two comfortable chairs and just enjoyed an hour together. The two women were at ease together, it was as if they had known each other forever.

There was just two days left on the cruise and both would be at sea. Ciara suggested that they meet up again before they reach their final port and go their separate ways. However, she didn't feel well the next morning and really wished that she was at home. Ciara got out of bed to go to the bathroom and immediately felt ill, she just made it there in time to vomit. Now she knew that she was unwell and should stay in bed. Bill was full of concern for her and asked what she had eaten the previous day, fish perhaps. Ciara agreed that must be it. She persuaded Bill to go and have his swim and enjoy their second last day of the holiday. She assured him that she just had a tummy upset and would be ok. She promised to call him if she needed him.

On his way to the pool, Bill met Sally. She asked if Ciara was out and about. He told her of Ciara's upset stomach. Sally asked if she could go and see her. Bill phoned Ciara to see if that would be ok, then he gave the code for their cabin to Sally and off she went.

There was a gentle knock, then Sally came in. She put her arms around the young woman and hugged her tightly. "A cup of tea?" she asked Ciara.

"No thanks," answered Ciara weakly.

"How are you feeling, lovey?" Sally asked.

"A bit better now. It must be something I ate yesterday. I don't know what exactly it could have been. I can usually eat what I like without any ill effects."

Sally sat on the bed beside her and said, "Did I tell you what I did before starting the company?"

"No," said Ciara.

"Well, I was a nurse and I know a bit about morning sickness."

Ciara started to protest, but Sally put her finger to her mouth, signalling to Ciara to listen. "When did you have your last period?"

Ciara sat bolt upright. "W-what?" she started to stutter, then began to think about it. There was so much going on that she had not noticed, but it was a while ago. Then she remembered just before they went to Tramore and Bill did all the packing.

"Will I go and get a test kit for you?" she asked. Ciara nodded. As Sally reached the door, Bill entered.

"How is the patient?"

"No fear of her!" answered Sally. "I am going to the pharmacy to get her an antacid. She will be as right as rain in an hour or two." The older woman had taken over. "Off you go now, young man. I will look after her." Bill did as he was told.

Ciara laughed. "I have never seen him obey an order before."

Sally returned shortly with a paper bag. She took out a pack of antacids and left them on the side table, then the pregnancy test kit. Ciara went to the bathroom and performed the test. She didn't think for one minute that the test could be positive. But it was. She climbed into bed, curled up and began to cry. Sally made herself some tea and gave Ciara time to come to terms with the incredible news. She walked out on to the balcony with her tea, wishing they could have afforded a cabin like this. Then she looked at the beautiful young woman in the bed. 'Luxury is not the answer to everything,' she thought. Even though Ciara and Bill looked like the perfect couple, that apparently was not the case.

Sally came back in and sat down. She spoke softly, as if she was addressing a child. "I take it, this is not good news then?"

Ciara shook her head. She was a mess now and looked it. She was nothing like the woman in the red dress, with the gorgeous husband. "I can't tell Bill. He will know straight away." Sally didn't want to push her to talk – she kept silent. "If I can just get through today and tomorrow without him knowing," she looked at the older woman for an answer. If only Kate were here, she would know what to do.

"Well, if you don't want your husband to know yet, eat snacks, little and often. Ask for breakfast in bed tomorrow morning that should get you through until you get home."

Home. Where was that? She could not go back with Bill. What was she to do? Would life ever be simple again?

Chapter 22

Sally left Ciara to go and find her husband and let him know where she was. Before she left, she promised to come back. By the time she did, Ciara was out of bed and feeling better physically, if not emotionally. They went out on to the balcony and sat down.

"Now lovey, if you feel like talking you can, or we can just sit here if you like. Sometimes unloading to a stranger is more comfortable than telling a loved one." Sally stopped talking.

It was a while before Ciara said, "Oh Sally, I have made such a mess of my life, and this is the last straw. It should be such a happy time in my life and in Bill's. He has wanted a baby ever since we got married. This baby is not his. Anyway, I don't love him anymore. He booked this cruise to try and get back what we had before. It didn't work, not for me, and now I am pregnant with another man's child. How on earth do I tell him all this?"

Sally was shocked. What a mess! She liked Ciara on meeting her, but now she was feeling sorry for her husband. She reached across and put her hand over Ciara's. "And this other man, the father of your baby, do you love him?"

The answer came in an instant. "Yes, very much."

"Do you have a future with this other man?"

"No, I don't," she said sadly. She couldn't bring herself to say that he's a priest and that they had a one-night stand. Just saying it to herself, made her feel cheap.

"First things first," said Sally. "You should say nothing about the child until you and Bill are at home. Can you do that?"

"Yes," answered Ciara.

"Do you have someone at home to go to when you do tell him?" Ciara nodded. "That's good. Now it's best if you pretend to be unwell until then. Stay here, eat small but often, breakfast in bed. If you are sick in the morning again, he will be suspicious."

Ciara sat back in the chair and looked up to the sky. Thank God for Sally. Without her help she could not have held it together for the next few days, and it was going to be bad enough for poor Bill when they got home. She felt sick again, this time it was for her husband and what she had done to him. He had done all he could to get her love back, now he was going to hate her and her child. Her and David's child. Suddenly she realised that Sally was talking to her. "Sorry Sally. I was not listening."

They were both startled when Bill entered the cabin. Smiling, he went over to Ciara and kissed her on the cheek. "How are you now, darling? Feeling better?"

She looked up and smiled. "Yes, thank you. I'm feeling much better. Thanks to this lovely lady who used to be a nurse."

Bill was immediately impressed. "Oh, that is a stroke of good luck. Do you think she should she see a doctor?"

Sally stood up and looked at Bill. "No, she just needs to relax and eat small meals." She winked at Bill. "Breakfast in bed would help. She'll be right as rain in no time, now I must go and see if my husband has found a new woman," laughed Sally.

"I can't thank you enough for looking after my wife. Will we see you and your husband for dinner tonight?"

"Looking forward to it!"

He turned to Ciara. "Will you be up to joining us sweetheart?"

"Not sure yet. Perhaps I will have something small."

"Just ask for a table for four for Parrish," he said as he closed the door behind Sally Taylor.

Consumed with guilt now, Ciara continued to sit on the balcony. She didn't trust her legs to keep her upright. If only it were Bill's child or if she could pretend it was, but as they hadn't had sex in such a long time, there was no possibility of letting him think that. Looking out to sea, Ciara wished that she could be swallowed up by it and never have to explain what she had done. They were at sea again tomorrow. How was she going to manage?

Chapter 23

Ciara had been never as happy as she was to land back in Ireland and be finished with the sham of a holiday. It was late, and they were staying with Kate and Marcus until tomorrow. When she hugged her sister, she never wanted to let go, and Kate picked up on it.

"So," said Marcus, "did you two have fun?"

Bill gave them a full account of the ship and all it had to offer, who they met and their shopping trips. Meanwhile Kate had a bottle of wine and was filling glasses, she left one in front of her sister, but she opted for a cup of tea. Kate expressed surprise at this, but Bill was quick to tell them how Ciara was a bit off-colour in the last few days.

"Actually," said Ciara, "I am going to bed, if that's ok?" She picked up her cup and left them chatting. After about ten minutes, Kate went to check on her sister and found her fast asleep, or pretending to be, thought Kate. Something was not right with these two and Bill hadn't a clue. He acted as if everything was back to normal and they had returned to where they were before Father Magee came on the scene.

The next morning the two men left early to go to some event or other. Kate could only think of her sister. As soon as they left, she went straight to the room where her sister was still pretending to sleep. She stood over the bed and said in a loud voice, "Come on, I know you are not asleep. And you are going to have to talk to me at some stage. It might as well be now. We are alone."

With that, Ciara sat up in the bed. "Can I have some tea and toast, please Kate?"

"What am I, your servant? Get out of that bed, and we will have some breakfast in the kitchen."

"I can't," said Ciara weakly. "If I get out of bed, I will be sick."

Kate was losing patience with her now. "Sick? What do you mean? What is wrong with you Ciara?" This was not a question – it was a demand. Kate sat on the bed. "Start talking."

Ciara lay back against the pillows and put her hand across her stomach. "I'm pregnant, Kate."

Without a word, Kate got up and went to make tea and toast for her sister. Kate's mind was all over the place. She knew that they wanted a baby and that Bill wanted it more than Ciara, but why had she not told him? She set the tray on the bed beside her sister, who had not moved since she left. "Why haven't you told Bill?"

"It's not his baby."

"Whose baby is it then?" shouted Kate. Suddenly the penny dropped. "Of course! It's Father Magee's. God Ciara, when you fuck up, you go all out, don't you? Your marriage is over, and you are having a baby with the parish priest!" Kate left and banged the door after her.

She returned an hour later when she calmed down. Ciara really was asleep this time, and when she woke up, she realised that this was the best sleep she'd had in quite a while. She felt relieved to have told her sister about the baby and to be away from her husband.

Kate was still angry but more composed now. "When are you going to tell Bill? Are you going home with him this evening?"

"I am not ready to tell him yet, Kate. If I could stay for a few days, that would be great. I have to decide what to do, and I need to be away from him while I make that decision."

"What are you talking about, Ciara?"

"Come and sit down, sis. Look at my circumstances. I can't go back to Bill. I have no job and no place to live. I cannot bring this child into my world. I have nothing to give it. If I have a termination, I can go back to Dublin and build a new life for myself and get a divorce. Bill deserves that too. It's not just my life I have destroyed, it's his also. I will not take a penny from him," said Ciara.

"There is one person you have not mentioned here. What about the father of the child?"

"He is in England, and I have not heard from him."

"So how do you know where he is then?"

"His sister told me."

Kate was pacing the room now. "Ciara, you didn't do this all on your own. Why should your life be the only one to be turned upside down?"

"Because Bill is innocent in all of this and David is a priest for life."

"Pity he didn't think of that the night he fell into bed with you. Well, let us talk about the baby then. It didn't ask for any of this. It has a strong, healthy mother and father, surely it deserves to have a shot at life?"

Ciara jumped out of bed. "Stop it, Kate!" she shouted. "I can't think about that. I just can't."

"Well, you are not exactly penniless. You have a wealthy husband, and savings I'm sure. We could help you, and Father Magee has a duty to the child. All I am asking, Ciara, is that you think about it? Don't do anything that you might regret for the rest of your life. Think about when the baby was conceived. How you felt then. Think about David. If you met him, could you tell him that you had his child terminated? Just think about it. Please. Let Bill go home, and you stay here. You can talk to him when you are ready, if you are sure that your marriage is over. Say nothing about the pregnancy."

"Ok," said Ciara, too tired to argue anymore.

"Come on, we will get your bags from the Jeep and get you settled. We will go down to Ballyfauna when he is at work and get more of your stuff. He is not going to be happy; you do know that?"

"Not happy! I dread to think what he will be like."

Happy enough to leave his wife in good hands, Bill went home earlier, but before doing so, he kissed Ciara on the lips as if to show the others that they were back on track.

Ciara slept soundly that night. It was her first good night's sleep in a long time. Now that her mind was made up, at least about her marriage. No pretending with Bill, when she saw him again, she would tell him that it was over. She no longer loved him, at least that was one certainty in her life. She would think about the rest of it tomorrow.

Chapter 24

It was mid-morning when she woke. Marcus and Kate were at work. She got out of bed without thinking and immediately was reminded that she was pregnant. She made it to the bathroom. Then went back to bed and made herself comfortable. She needed to find out how long this morning sickness was going to last. Then she let her mind wander... if David was with her, would he bring her tea in bed? Would he be excited about the baby? She wondered if he had ever wanted to be a parent, if he had ever wanted to be married. Sadly, she knew very little about the father of her unborn child. Would he blame her for what happened between them? Was it her fault? She should not have gone to his house. She should have said no, when he kissed her. She was married.

His kisses came back to her, and she remembered it as if it had happened only yesterday – that feeling of closeness she felt as they lay together in his bed. She would give anything to be back there just one more time and to tell him that she loved him. She began to cry and felt the pain of loss, it was as if he had died. She knew that she would never see him again. Ciara put her hand on her stomach and for the first time thought of the baby that was growing in there and the fact that it was David's child. How could she have thought of getting rid of it?

Instantly she knew that she couldn't do that. She was going to have David's baby. They would manage somehow.

There was a light knock on the door. Marcus poked his head around. "Are you ok, Ciara?"

In a much lighter voice, she answered. "Yes, thank you, Marcus. Coming down now shortly."

"Ok, I will put the coffee on," and he was gone. Marcus was pouring two cups of coffee. Ciara could smell it and knew that she could not drink it. Seeing her reaction, Marcus asked what was wrong.

"I seem to have gone off coffee, Marcus," she giggled.

"That's unusual," he said. "When did that happen?"

"When we were on the ship," answered Ciara.

"It's not just my coffee, then?"

"No, it's coffee in general, something to do with the smell."

"You seem to be feeling better today," he smiled.

"Yes. My mind is much clearer now. Marcus, I have to tell you something, and it's difficult. You and

Bill get on very well, but this has been coming for a while now and can't be put off any longer. The marriage is over, but I've not told him yet. Kate has offered me some time here, and I hope that's ok with you."

Marcus reached across and caught her hand. "You know that you are always welcome here, Ciara, and for as long as you need."

"Thanks, Marcus. Now that I am confessing, I may as well keep going."

Looking a bit concerned, he said. "Go on."

"I am pregnant."

"Wow!" said Marcus. "Have you told Bill yet?"

"No, it's David's baby."

Marcus appeared to be in shock and was stuck for a comment. "Are you ok, Ciara?"

"I will be once I tell Bill."

They heard the door closing and knew that Kate was home. She came into the kitchen and did not look at all happy. Marcus was wise enough to leave the sisters with each other.

"So, you got out of bed. That's a start, I suppose." Kate was obviously very cross with Ciara and who could blame her. Even sisters have limits and when you come with as much baggage as Ciara.

"Have you given any more thought to the baby?" said Kate. It sounded more like an accusation than a question.

Ciara came and sat at the table and said, "Yes, I have. I'm keeping it."

Kate's face lit up, she came around to where her sister was sitting and hugged her. "Oh, thank God for that! You will be a wonderful mother, and I will be an auntie. Oh, Ciara, I am so happy for you and for us too."

"I just have Bill to deal with. And I'm not looking forward to that. He will be furious. He was sure that all we needed was a holiday and some fancy clothes. I was tempted to go along with it until I discovered that I was pregnant. And you know how he felt about David and that was when he didn't know that we had slept together." Ciara cringed.

"You don't have to tell him if the marriage is over."

"Kate, would it be awful of me to tell him in a letter?"

"Yes, you need to do it face-to-face. Are you sure that you want to do it now?"

"Yes, I don't have a choice. He'll know that it could not be his child. We have not been together like that in a long time, not until the cruise. Even then I was only making an effort to save our marriage. It didn't work. There is nothing to save. I just don't want to be with him anymore. I know that he will be very angry with me for showing him up as a man who couldn't keep his wife."

Kate was taken aback at this statement by her sister. "Surely, that's not what he will feel. You are his wife, not a car."

"I am his possession. I could not tell you that while we were married, but I have known it for quite a while, and if I were not leaving him, I probably wouldn't tell you now. Now all that is left is for me to tell Bill."

Chapter 25

"I am shocked, sis. I thought you two were perfect together," said Kate.

Ciara laughed. "And you a professional! Just goes to show, all you know about marriage is what the couple decides to share with you."

"So, have you been unhappy with him all this time?"

"No, it was only while spending time with David that I began to see how fragile our marriage really was and how controlling Bill is. The cruise confirmed that for me." Ciara went on to tell Kate about the red dress and the necklace.

"I thought that it was cute, the way he could pack your bag," said Kate.

"It was as if he was packing for himself and he needed me to look perfect beside him. I never wanted or needed expensive things, which is just as well now," she laughed.

Kate took a deep breath since it seems to be confession time. "There is something I am going to tell you. Maybe I should put the kettle on first."

"Ok, tea for me, please," said Ciara. "Looks like junior here doesn't like coffee."

When they were settled down with two cups of tea, Kate said, "You know how we always said that we didn't want children?"

Ciara nodded.

"That's not true. We have no children because we can't have any."

Ciara went to reach out to her sister and Kate raised her hand. "You see, that is why we decided to say we didn't want them, to avoid the sympathy. It's also why I saw red last night when you talked about termination." This time it was Kate in tears. "I'm glad that you are pregnant. I was afraid that you might be the same as me, unable to have children. Now that you have told me about Bill, I'm very glad that this baby is not his." Between laughter and tears, she caught her sister's hand. "Oh Ciara, we are going to have a baby. I am delighted!"

Marcus had come in unnoticed by the two women, who were engrossed in conversation.

"I am glad that you are both happy," he said sincerely, "but when are you going to tell your husband? You know that he will be devastated by this news, Ciara?"

"Yes Marcus, I know he will, and he will be furious. And for that reason alone, I ask you both if I could tell him here."

Marcus looked to his wife for guidance here, and Kate nodded her agreement. "It seems to me, Marcus, that we don't know Bill as well as we thought we did. I believe that it is best if she does it here."

Later that night Ciara got a phone call from Bill. She went into the bedroom to take the call. He asked how she was feeling.

"Very well, thanks," she replied. "How are you?"

"Great. Looking forward to you coming home."

Silence.

"Ciara, are you still there?"

"Yes," she answered quietly. "Bill, I am staying here."

"For how long?"

"For good. I am not coming back to you. Our marriage is over. I am sorry. I really thought we might be able to get it back when we went on holiday, but now I am sure that it's over, Bill."

His voice was raised. "Don't be ridiculous, Ciara! You are my wife, and this is your home. I want you home here tomorrow," and he hung up.

Ciara was shaken when she returned to sit with the others. "I knew it. He is furious and ordered me home tomorrow."

"Ok," said Marcus, "he knows now. He will calm down overnight, and you can talk to him again tomorrow. You can't keep him in the dark any longer. It's not fair. You need to stay calm and look after yourself and the baby too." Marcus got a footstool for her, and the three of them sat down to watch television.

About an hour later, there was a loud knock on the door. Kate jumped up to see who it was. Bill burst in, totally ignoring Kate. If she had not been told by her sister, that he could be like this, she wouldn't have believed it. Without greeting Marcus or Kate, he stood there looking at his wife.

"Come on Ciara, let's go home." He kicked the footstool from under her feet and went to grab her.

Marcus jumped up and shouted. "Bill, what are you doing?"

He looked at Marcus with fury in his face. "I am taking my wife home, where she belongs."

"By all means take your wife home – if that's where she wants to go. Otherwise, leave her alone."

Ciara stood up. "Bill, we need to talk." She walked towards the bedroom with an enraged Bill in hot pursuit. Ciara sat down while Bill continued to stand over her, glaring down at her.

"What is this nonsense about you not coming home? I just took you on a cruise that cost me a fortune, and now you tell me that you are staying here.

Well, I have news for you, lady. You are not going to make a show of me. Now get your things and come with me."

"Bill, get it into your head. It's over. The marriage is finished. I don't love you any more."

Marcus entered the room. "Come on now, Bill. She's told you she wants to stay here and that's that."

Ciara thought that he was going to hit Marcus. The two men stood facing each other.

"She is my wife, Marcus, and she is coming home with me now."

"Yes, Bill, Ciara is your wife, but you don't own her. If she wants to stay here, she is welcome to."

Bill was beyond listening. Once again, he went to grab her hand, and Marcus shouted. "Leave her alone, she's pregnant!"

Bill stopped in his tracks, looking from one to the other. "Pregnant? You can't be! It's not possible."

Kate heard what her husband had said, and she came into the room to protect her sister. "Come on, Bill. It's time to leave. Marcus, should I call the police?" He didn't answer.

"Pregnant? That can't be right. Ciara, are you pregnant?" The two women were now standing at one side of the bed, and Marcus was closer to Bill.

Marcus answered for Ciara. "Yes Bill, she is."

Suddenly all the anger was gone, and Bill sat on the bed. He put his head in his hands and said quietly, "That fucking priest!" Then he looked at his wife for confirmation. She nodded. "It was already too late when I got rid of him? I should have done it sooner."

Chapter 26

M arcus repeated Bill's words. "When you got rid of him? You did that? You put out that rumour about an innocent man?"

"You call him innocent? My wife is having his baby, when she should be carrying my child! That was all I ever asked of her. The only reason I married her. And I gave her everything!" shouted Bill.

Marcus was enraged. "How could I have been so wrong about you, Bill? Come on, get out of our home and don't come back. We will get a solicitor for Ciara, and you can deal with each other through him." Ciara barely recognised the man who walked out of the bedroom and out the front door. Whatever happened to the self-confident handsome man she had married and why did it take until now for her to realise who he really was.

The three of them went to the living room and just sat there without a word.

"Is this all my fault?" Ciara asked.

Marcus was quick to speak. "No, Ciara."

"What now?" asked Kate, and they looked from one to the other.

"I don't know," said Marcus. "What Bill did is criminal. I will have to speak to my solicitor. Anyway, there is nothing we can do tonight." Marcus took his wife's hand. "You are a good sister, Kate. I am a very fortunate man to have you as my wife." They kissed each other briefly. Then looking at Ciara sympathetically. "I am sorry that things didn't work for you and Bill. He clearly is not the man we thought he was. You deserve better. Now you need to think about looking after yourself and your baby."

"Have you heard from David?"

"No," said Ciara sadly, "and I don't think I ever will. Bill saw to that."

"Well," said Marcus, "he will have to be told where the rumour about him came from. I will talk to the solicitor tomorrow. And I will ask him about your rights, Ciara – if you want me to?"

"Thank you, but I doubt that I have rights now that I am having a baby outside of the marriage."

"We'll see," said Marcus as he stood up to leave the sisters. "I am off to bed."

Kate moved closer to her sister and put her arm around her shoulder.

"I knew it," said Ciara.

"Knew what?"

"That he never loved me. I realised it that day in Tramore, but I tried to ignore it. I feel like such a fool."

"No, he is the fool, not realising what he had in you. Now try to put him out of your mind." Then she put her hand on Ciara's stomach. "Imagine a baby is growing in there! I wonder if it's a boy or a girl? I am free tomorrow; do you want to go to a doctor and get confirmation and a due date?"

"Ok, let's do that," smiled Ciara.

"Then we can go look at baby clothes," said Kate with a laugh. "Now off to bed with you and have a good sleep. The hardest part is done."

Ciara got into bed thinking that she could not possibly sleep considering what had taken place in this room earlier, then her thoughts turned to David and what her husband had done to him. She wondered where he was and how he would feel about being a father, should she tell him? He had, after all, given his life to the church, which meant that he did not want a family. Did he have the right to know, or would she destroy his life further?

The following morning, it was Bill that she thought about and he looked very different now. All his attractiveness had gone. In fact, she thought, it was never there except on the surface. Sure, he was great to look at, but that is where it ends. She realised now that she had been carefully selected to be the wife, the mother and the lady of the manor and to her shame, he knew that he could control her.

Luckily for her, fate had stepped in, and even though she was going to be a single mother, her child had a good father, and with a shock, she remembered David's sister and his parents. Her child had an extended family, not that they would ever see them.

Kate knocked on the door. "I have made an appointment for you with a doctor at the hospital."

"Ok sis, I will be there shortly."

Kate introduced her to a doctor called Hana. Then she looked back to her sister and said, "Do you want to book in here to give birth?"

Ciara laughed at her sister. "Let's make sure that I am pregnant first."

"Ok then, off you go. Thanks, Hana," Kate called after them. The scan was carried out, and the doctor confirmed that Ciara Parrish was indeed seven weeks pregnant and the baby would arrive at the end of April. She lay there looking at the screen, thinking how she had David's baby was growing inside her. She shed a tear and wished with all her heart that he was here to see it.

Hana never mentioned the father, and Ciara assumed that her sister had filled the doctor in on the state of her marriage. When she was dressed and ready, she was asked if she wanted to book into Naas General for the birth and the next scan in eight weeks.

Kate was over the moon that she was going to be an aunty. "Come on, let's go shopping and start looking at baby stuff!" she said and gave a loud laugh.

Ciara gave her sleeve a tug. "Not today, Kate. I'm not in the mood. Sorry."

In her excitement, Kate forgot that this was no ordinary situation and that her sister's head was all over the place. "Ok. Do you want to go straight home?"

"Yes, please. I have a lot on my mind."

"Do you want to talk about it?"

"What will my baby's name be? I won't call it Parrish. I can't call it Magee. What will I do, sis?" The girls were sitting in the car.

Kate drew her sister close. "You don't have to decide that for a while yet, sis. You could always go back to being Connolly for you and the child." With that, Ciara cheered up. Yes, that is a good idea. Maybe a little male Connolly.

Chapter 27

After work that day, Marcus went to see a solicitor, who was also a friend and explained the situation to him. The solicitor said to leave it with him, he would get back to him as soon as possible. As good as his word, Marcus was not long home when his phone rang.

Later as the three of them were having dinner, he told them what the solicitor had suggested. On behalf of the three of them, who had witnessed Bill's confession about Father Magee, the solicitor would write to the bishop and tell him what they now knew to be the truth. Then he would contact David, as he would be the one to take action against Bill, or not. If he wanted to go to court to clear his name, he would need all three of them as witnesses.

Ciara thought she was going to faint. She felt cold and shivery. The very idea of going to court to stand between the two men. Marcus noticed the look on her face. He reached for a throw, put it around her shoulders and led her to the sofa. "Relax Ciara, it may never come to that, and if you are not able for it, we can go and get you excused on medical grounds."

"When do you think that all of this might happen, Marcus?"

"I have no idea, and you do not need to worry about it anymore. It was very stupid of me to think that you could be a witness. I don't know what I was thinking."

Kate put a pillow under her sister's head and went back to finish dinner. When she looked again, Ciara was sleeping.

Father David Magee was told in a phone conversation with the bishop's office that information had come from a solicitor in Naas. He was now clear of the accusation against him and he was free to resume his duties. He had an issue with the church now. He had plenty of time to think in the last few weeks. He felt abandoned by the catholic church, sent into exile, ordered to leave, without even being able to say goodbye to his family. Everything became clear to him after he had been falsely accused of being a paedophile and he was thrown to the wolves. He was never even asked by the bishop if he was guilty.

If the solicitor was from Naas, then it must have come from Marcus Langley. He was the only person he knew from that part of the country. He immediately phoned Marcus to ask how he had found the person who hated him enough to start a rumour like this.

He was shocked but was not surprised at the name of the person who had put the word out, and he wondered what to do now. Taking Bill Parrish to court would set the record straight, but what about the effect that would have on Ciara. She was his priority, and he wouldn't hurt her for the world. He had never loved a woman before. Yes, he had been drawn to one or two ladies in the past, but he had resisted the temptation. This, however, was different. She was different. She was the reason that he was thinking of leaving the church and going abroad to do some charity work to try and forget her. How could he ever forget that night when they had made love like two people possessed. It was the most wonderful and the most painful of memories. If only they had been able to continue working together.

He could go to Ballyfauna to see her one last time, but that would not be fair to her if she still felt as he did. He wondered if she knew what her husband had done to get rid of him. What sort of man was he really? Was he a good husband? Did she love him?

He was sick at the thought that she was living and sleeping with Bill Parrish, but he had no right to come between a man and his wife, nor was he free to do so, even though he was leaving the priesthood.

His thoughts were interrupted by the phone. It was the bishop, offering him a new parish. There were no words of apology for what he had been through. David listened to his boss, but only heard some of what he was saying. He was now clear in his mind about his future.

When the phone conversation was over, he put pen to paper to request that he be laicized. He had no idea how long this might take or if indeed his request would be granted. All he knew for sure was that he was in love with a woman and had broken his vow of celibacy. That would make him a failed priest and unable in his conscience to continue in a ministry. With that thought, he sealed the letter ready for posting.

David Magee felt a weight lift off his shoulders. He was free even though the church could deny his request, they could not force him to perform clerical duties. Now he must go and tell his parents. He knew that they would be disappointed, but it had to be done. He would ask Mary to be there. She was good to have around during challenging situations, and this was one. His mother was a deeply religious woman and having her son in the priesthood was very important to her.

Chapter 28

Ciara woke late the next morning. She was surprised to still be on the sofa and at having slept quite well there. The house was quiet, meaning that Kate and Marcus had already gone to work. She was glad to be alone. She needed time to think. Breakfast was necessary now that there was a baby to consider. A smile crossed her face as she thought of the new life inside her and rubbed her stomach, letting it know that it would be cherished, with or without its father. The big question now was whether she should contact David and tell him? Maybe she should have a chat with Kate first.

David would not be the first priest in Ireland to father a child. Though it would be a scandal if it were known and would not be good for any of them. Ciara also had to think of getting a job and a place of her own to live; none of which was going to be easy. A small apartment would suffice. Of course, it would have to have two bedrooms.

She sat back and laughed at the thought of all the rooms at Ivy Manor and the special place set aside for a nursery. Would Bill divorce her and marry again? Divorce was not something that she had thought about. There was a lot to think about.

The next thing she heard was the kitchen door close. Kate was home from work. Ciara had slept most of the day. The sisters began to prepare dinner and not long afterwards, Marcus arrived home. He mentioned that he had a missed call from Father David Magee. Ciara's heart skipped a beat at the very mention of his name.

During dinner the phone rang, and Marcus recognised the number. "David. Hello, how are you?"

"Very well thanks, Marcus. How are you and Kate?" Without waiting for an answer, David continued to thank Marcus for his help in clearing his name. "I have decided not to take action against him, but only because of Ciara. Besides I am going away in the next few days."

"Oh, where are you going to?" said Marcus.

"Africa to do some work with the poor. I have also made a big decision. I have requested that I be laicised, but that could take a while."

"So, big changes for you then, David," said Marcus.

"Yes, Marcus, changes come when you least expect them, and sometimes they can turn your life upside down."

"They certainly can, David." After a hasty farewell, Marcus put the phone down.

Kate and Ciara, sat at the dining table, their eyes fixed on Marcus.

"Well?" said Kate.

"That was David," said Marcus.

"Yes, we know. What did he say?" asked Kate.

"I'm not sure," said Marcus. "He is going to Africa."

Ciara gasped. "Africa! Why is he going there? Did he ask about me?"

"Yes, well, no. He mentioned you. He's not going to take Bill to court because it would upset you," said Marcus.

Kate poured a glass of wine for her husband, seeing his confusion after the call.

Ciara stood up. "He didn't even want to talk to me or ask for my phone number."

Kate stood up and put her arm around her sister. "Ciara, he didn't know that you are here. He thinks that you are at home with Bill."

"What am I to do? He is going away. I might never see him again!" she said glaring at her brother-in-law, as if it was all his fault. "Why didn't you tell him that I was here, carrying his child?"

"I didn't have time, Ciara. Plus, I didn't know if you wanted me to tell him or not. However, I do have his phone number, if you want to ring him. It's apparent that he cares for you, that's the reason he's not taking Bill to court for slander because it would be upsetting for you."

"I don't know what to do! Bill is getting away scot-free after what he did to David, and he is doing that for me?"

"Yes," said Marcus, "and he is leaving the priest-hood."

Ciara didn't know whether to laugh or cry at this bit of news. Now she knew that she needed to talk to him. Marcus wrote down the phone number and left it on the table in front of her. Picking up the piece of paper, was making a massive decision. She was going to call him, but it had to be in private. She walked to the bedroom. Once she was sitting on the bed, she began to key in the number, then cancelled the call. 'What if he is not interested in me or the baby? He might think that it's Bill's child. He has plans to go to Africa…'

Chapter 29

Kate and Marcus were in the kitchen waiting to see how the phone call went. When Ciara came back into the room, it looked like it did not go well.

"I couldn't do it," she announced, her lower lip trembling. She was close to tears.

"Well, someone is going to have to do it before it's too late!" declared Kate, clearly irritated at her husband and her sister.

Kate dialled the number. David answered. She summoned him to a meeting at their house. He began to ask why but she cut him off. "You must get here before you leave." With clear instructions as to how to find the house, she said goodbye and hung up. The two onlookers were shocked, neither one of them would have been able to achieve that.

"When is he coming here, Kate?" asked Ciara.

"I don't know. Before he leaves for Africa," replied Kate.

Ciara needed to be alone. She went to the bedroom. She was going to see him. She was going to see

David. The memory of that night came back, his kisses, their lovemaking, 'Oh my God, I wonder if he feels the same, or was it just a one-night stand. The baby! Will he believe that it is his? Will he want a DNA test?' These, and other thoughts ran constantly through her head.

There was a gentle knock on the door, and Kate entered carrying a cup of tea. "No point overthinking things now, sis. It is what it is, Ciara. No amount of worry is going to change that. You just have to deal with him when he gets here. I suggest a good night's sleep. You do want to look your best when you see him, don't you?"

Ciara hugged her sister and thanked her for making contact with David.

It was late when Kate and Marcus went to bed that night. They were settling down for a good night's sleep when Marcus's phone rang. It was a colleague at the hospital.

"Hello Marcus, sorry to disturb you, but we have a patient here. He was brought in after an accident, and your number is the last contact on his mobile phone. His name is Father David Magee. A friend of yours?"

Marcus whispered to Kate what he had just been told. They decided not to tell Ciara yet.

"I better go in and see how he is. He must have been on his way here," said Marcus.

Kate lay there after her husband had gone and hoped that David was alright. She was the one that told him to come here.

It was after three o'clock when her phone rang.

"How is he?" she asked.

"Not good. I'm afraid he's in a coma," said Marcus.

Kate jumped out of bed. "Oh my God! Marcus, this is my fault!"

Marcus was firm. "It is not anyone's fault, Kate. It was an accident. Now, do we tell Ciara or not? We have to think of her condition and just how upset she is going to be. Let's wait until tomorrow morning. We might know more about him by then. I have seen his phone and the name Mary is in it, I presume that's his sister. I will ring her now. The family will have to be informed."

Mary decided not to tell her parents until she knew more about David's injuries. She left immediately to travel to Naas General Hospital. It was four o'clock in the morning, and the road would be quiet. It would take about two and a half hours to get there. Thank God Ciara's brother-in-law worked there and would meet her when she arrived. This is the same man who helped clear David's name. She wondered if he was going to meet Marcus Langley when the accident happened, or perhaps he knew someone else in the area. Ciara was the next person who came to her mind. Mary decided to ring her tomorrow when she knew more.

Chapter 30

Marcus was having a cat nap in the waiting area and had given instructions that he was to be called immediately when Mary Magee arrived.

"Excuse me, Mr Langley? Miss Magee is here."

Marcus had been in a deep sleep. It took him a few seconds to recall Mary and why he was here sleeping in a chair.

"Mary, please sit down. Your brother was involved in a very bad accident," began Marcus.

Mary cut in. "Is he alive?"

"Yes, he is. But we don't know the full extent of his injuries yet. You will have to be patient for a little longer. Come with me, and I will get you a proper cup of tea, then I will go and get an update." Marcus took her to the staff canteen and left her in the care of a kind nurse while he went to talk to his colleagues.

David had a broken arm and a severe wound to his right leg but they had not found the reason for him being in a coma yet. Tests were being carried out, and they just had to wait and see.

Before returning to Mary Magee, Marcus decided to ring Kate, who was up by now and waiting for his call. She would want an update to tell her sister.

Ciara was already up and showered. She was taking great care with her appearance today in the hope that she would meet David. While trying to decide on a pair of earrings, her sister gave a light knock on the door and came in. Without turning around, Ciara said, "What do you think?"

Kate sat on the bed and didn't answer. "Come and sit down, sis. I have something to tell you. It's about David."

Ciara held her breath. "What about him?"

Kate took hold of her sister's hand. "He was in an accident last night. He was on his way here when it happened. They took him to Naas General. Marcus has been there all night. All we know is that David is in a coma. His sister is there with him. We decided not to tell you during the night because there was nothing you could do, and you needed your sleep."

Ciara jumped to her feet. "Where is he? Can I go to the hospital? I have to go to him! Could he die?"

"Hold on now, Ciara. You won't be allowed in, not now. All we can do is wait for Marcus to ring us," said Kate.

"Who rang Mary?"

"Marcus did. He got her number from David's phone," said Kate.

"Perhaps I should ring her?" fretted Ciara.

"I don't think so, Ciara. How would you explain your interest and you being here in Naas? She believes that you are happily married down in Ballyfauna and this is not the time to tell her. She has enough to deal with right now."

"Kate, I have to see him! What if he dies and I never get to tell him that he is going to be a dad?"

Just then Kate's phone rang. It was her husband. She walked away from her sister as she spoke, but Ciara followed like a child. "Is he alright?"

Feeling weak and light headed, Ciara sat down and prayed, not something she would typically do, but for this man she would do anything, pray to anybody. Kate said goodbye to Marcus and returned to sit beside her sister.

Chapter 31

"There is no change in David's condition. He is no better, nor any worse. The next forty-eight hours are critical. His doctor is in constant contact with Marcus, and we will hear immediately if there is any change. Sorry sweetheart, but we have to wait and see what happens. He also told me that the bishop's secretary was there. They heard about the accident and are wondering why he was driving to Naas late at night. Mary Magee was asking the same question. Marcus has not enlightened them," said Kate. "Now there is something we need you to consider, Ciara. Marcus wants to know if Mary Magee could come here to stay with us, but only if you are ok with it. You will have to remember that she probably knows nothing about you and David. What do you think?" asked Kate.

Ciara was delighted to help in any way she could and having Mary here would make her feel closer to him. Kate messaged her husband and to say yes, invite Mary to stay. She also asked if she should go and collect her.

On the drive back from the hospital, Kate didn't mention that her sister was also staying with them. Mary was surprised and delighted to see Ciara. A familiar face was just what she needed, someone who knew her brother.

Mary thanked them for all that they had done to clear David's name. "He has not told me who started the vicious rumour in the first place, but he is not taking action against them, for personal reasons he said. My brother's life seems to have changed a lot since the day we all met in Tramore. He was due to go to Africa tomorrow. He and I went to see our parents yesterday, but what brought him up this side of the country last night? I have no idea what that was about."

Marcus came in and interrupted Mary, mid-sentence, for which Kate was grateful.

She wasn't ready to admit that she was the person who had summoned David Magee to Nass. Of course, she was not to know that he would take the journey that very night. He must have guessed that it had to do with Ciara. Kate was feeling tired, from being awake all night and carrying guilt for keeping things from Mary. If she told her that he was coming to see her, then she would have to say why she had asked him to come.

Marcus and Kate left for work early the next morning, leaving the other two ladies in bed. Marcus left a note for Mary. He had been on to the hospital, and there was no change in David's condition. On the drive to work, Kate decided to stop thinking about the issues surrounding her sister. It will all work out as it is meant to, as she told her clients regularly.

Mary was up before Ciara and had ordered a taxi to go to the hospital, as her car was still there.

"Oh," said Ciara, "I would have taken you there myself."

"No, Ciara. You have all done enough for me. Thank you very much," said Mary.

There was a newspaper on the sofa, she picked it up without thinking and was shocked by David's picture staring out at her with the story of the crash. She gasped as she dropped the newspaper and sat down. Then she picked it up again slowly as if it was going to hurt her, and it did. Just sitting there looking at him for the first time since the night they had been intimate, hurt her so much. 'Oh, David, I have missed you so much,' she said to herself and her tears spilled on to the picture. 'Now you are just a few miles from me, and I can't go to you. I want to sit beside you and hold your hand and tell you our news.' Joining her hands in prayer, Ciara cried out, "Please let him live, for our child and for me. Please, God. I love him so much."

When she was all cried out and still in the same spot on the sofa, she picked the paper up again and began to read the story of the accident. It said that he was

Father David Magee from Ballyfauna, County Wicklow. How could they! They had taken him from Ballyfauna after Bill had slandered him? He was in a coma all because of her. If he had never met her, none of this would have happened to him.

Chapter 32

She went to her bedroom and got into bed fully dressed. She had to think, but her head was bursting. It was Marcus who woke her, she had slept for a long time and was dazed when he came and put his hand on her arm.

"Are you alright, Ciara?" he asked.

Ciara looked at her brother-in-law as if to say, 'I am not fucking alright!'. "How is he, Marcus? When can I see him?"

"There is no change. Sorry, Ciara, I wish I had better news. Mary is with him and a priest from the bishop's office; O'Donnell, I think. Not a very nice chap. I think Mary would be better off without him. He asked me how I knew David, I told him that I met him at a race meeting. He can mind his own business," said Marcus, as he nudged Ciara playfully. "His parents are coming up from Cork tomorrow, just for the day. They can only go in one at a time anyway. I will try to get you in to see him in the next few days if he stays as he is now. Some people remain in a coma for a while. It is neither good nor bad, but while he is in intensive care, it is not easy to get you in there. Come and have a cup of tea and we will make dinner for Kate and Mary."

While preparing dinner, Marcus said, "Ciara, what are we going to tell Mary Magee? We have some big secrets here."

"I don't know. I saw it clearly today for the first time. It's all because of me. Maybe I should come clean, make a full confession, get you and Kate out of this mess," said Ciara.

Mary arrived home before Kate but planned to go back again and maybe stay the night at her brother's side. Marcus persuaded her to have dinner before going back. She didn't talk much during dinner. Ciara asked if there was anything she could do to help her. To her surprise, Mary said, "Yes, Ciara, would you please do some shopping for me? I know that he is going to wake up and when he does, he will need some pyjamas, slippers and a dressing gown."

Never thinking that she would be in the men's department of a shop, looking for clothes for David, despite the circumstances, Ciara was excited. There was no problem with the size. She lovingly picked up things that she would like to see on him. When she had everything on Mary's list, there was one item missing. Underwear, so off with her to get socks and boxers.

If asked how she knew what type he wore, well, she would have to lie.

The next morning, Mary came to the house early. She had some breakfast, a shower and changed her clothes. Their parents were coming to visit, she didn't seem very glad that they were arriving. Ciara asked if they were staying for a few days, and she could see that the other woman got upset as she answered, no.

"What's the problem, Mary?" asked Ciara.

"I don't know how to tell you this, or even if I should," said Mary.

"Go on," said Ciara, "you can trust me."

"Well, on the day of the accident, my brother told our parents that he was leaving the church and going to Africa," said Mary. "They were furious and told him to get out and never come back. Now they are only coming here to please the church. To save face, as it were. The same reason that Father O'Donnell is there, hovering around like a concerned friend. Ciara?"

Ciara nodded.

"Do you know where David was going when the accident happened?" asked Mary.

Telling lies did not come easy to her. She did the only thing she could. "Yes, Mary, I do. He was coming here."

"He told me that he had met someone, and that's why he was going to Africa, to try to forget her. Do you know…?" With that, Mary's phone rang. "Yes, Marcus," she listened carefully, then said, "Ok, I'll come right away." She disconnected the call. "I must go to him, something has changed." Mary ran to the door, and it banged behind her.

Ciara wanted to run after her and shout, 'What about me? I love him too!' but now was not the time for any further confessions. Instead, she phoned Kate to see if she could find out what was happening to David.

Kate answered immediately. "I am coming to get you, ok?" On the way to the hospital Kate explained what Marcus had told her of David's condition. "There are some changes to his brain activity, the doctors are not sure what it means yet. That's why they called for Mary, and his parents are due to visit also. I am finished work for the day, and you can sit in my office. I know that you really want to see him, but you can't at the moment. I will see what I can do later." Ciara couldn't speak; she touched her sister's hand, by way of a thank you.

Chapter 33

When she arrived at the hospital, she immediately felt closer to him. Unbeknownst to Ciara, Kate had told a good friend who was a doctor, about her sister's situation. They were introduced, and Fiona sat down beside Ciara and asked her to roll up her sleeve. While measuring her blood pressure, she said, "We need to make sure that you and your baby are well taken care of, as well as the daddy. You have had a big shock and lots of stress. I am going to be taking care of you for a while. Now I want you to hop up on the couch and I can see how the baby is doing." Fiona listened to the heartbeat and then suggested a scan just to put her mind at rest.

Kate winked at her sister as she left the office. "Don't worry, I will call you if there is any news."

Ciara didn't see what Fiona was looking at, nothing much to see yet. Still looking at the monitor, she spoke to her child for the first time. "You keep going little one and with the help of God, your Dad will too. I love you both very much." Fiona made no attempt to stop her talking or crying. She was happy with mother and baby but would order a blood test and keep an eye on her until this stressful time has passed.

As they walked back to Kate's office, she spotted Mary Magee and some people with her. She assumed they must be David's parents. It was a good sign if they were chatting in the corridor and not by his side. This was confirmed by Kate when they reached the office. There had been a slight change, but it had disappeared again.

Kate stood and picked up her bag. "Now, ladies, we are going to have some lunch to nourish that little niece or nephew of mine," she said. Nudging her sister playfully, she said, "And Fiona and I are having a glass of wine."

Mary had not seen Ciara in the corridor. Ciara decided to call her to see if she was ok. Considering what she knew of their parents, it might be an awkward encounter. Mary didn't answer and Ciara left a message asking if she was alright.

Lunch was very pleasant, and there was a lot of baby talk as Fiona filled them in on her two boys and the joy of having them. Fiona was aware that Kate would like to have a family, but at the risk of upsetting her, Fiona was trying to take Ciara's mind off David for an hour. They had just ordered two coffees and one tea when the phone rang. It was an unknown number, but she answered it anyway. It was Mary, she was agitated. Ciara got up from the table, almost knocking it over in the process.

"Mary, what's wrong? Is it David?"

Eventually, she calmed down enough to say what had upset her. Mary said, "My mother stood at the end of the bed and told David that he had disgraced them. She was asked to leave immediately by the nurse. Now she wants to go without my father even seeing David!"

Knowing how her mother felt about a priest leaving the church. Mary had been sure that when she saw him, and all the equipment around the bed keeping her only son alive, it would soften her heart and she would be glad that he might live and come out of this. No such luck. She was more concerned about what the church and the neighbours would say.

"Do you want me to come to be with you?" asked Ciara.

"Oh, Ciara, that would be great! I can't do this on my own," said Mary sadly.

The three women went back to the unit where David was.

The family were outside ICU, and no one was talking. Mary introduced her parents to Ciara and Kate introduced Dr Fiona O'Connor. Fiona sat down beside Mrs Magee and began to speak with her about her son. Mary took her Dad by the arm and led him to

David's bedside. She wanted to stay with him, but the very stern looking nurse would have none of it.

The older man looked heartbroken as he lifted his son's limp hand and lowered his face to it. "Come on, son, this is no time to give up. You have a whole new life before you. Take no notice of your Mam. She will come around, she always does." Two doctors entered and asked him to leave.

When the door opened again, David's bed was wheeled out and down the corridor. They were told nothing about where they were taking him or for what. Fiona suggested that the family go and have something to eat, it might be a while before they could see him again. She had Mrs Magee by the hand and spoke to her in a low voice. Ciara did not hear what she said, but the older woman seemed much calmer now.

Mary looked at Ciara. "If I go with my parents, will you stay here please?"

"I will," said Ciara. "Go on, and I will call you when they come back."

They had only been gone for five minutes when a doctor in scrubs came and asked for Mary. Kate made the call, and Ciara sat there numb. This was like one long bad dream. She wished he was in Africa, safe and well.

They told Mary that her brother needed an operation to relieve pressure on his brain and asked her to sign the consent form, as his next of kin. Now they were back to waiting.

Marcus arrived and insisted that they all go home, and he would wait for information. They would tell him, and he would be in touch as soon as there was news.

It was nine o'clock the next day when Marcus rang. He said that the operation had been a success and there was every chance that David would make a full recovery. Ciara was no longer consumed with seeing him, she was just glad that he was alive.

The following week was difficult for all concerned. David's parents returned to Naas, and they took turns sitting at his bedside.

Ciara had forgotten about her eight-week scan until Kate reminded her. This should have been a very happy time, knowing that her child was growing inside her, but hard as she tried, David's recovery was all she could think of.

Chapter 34

I t was Friday morning when Mary phoned. Their mother was at David's bedside when her son began to move ever so slightly and was trying to say something. Mrs Magee could not understand what he was saying, but Mary thought it was Ciara. The older woman asked who Ciara was. She had not made the connection.

Finally, it was Ciara's time to go and see him.

Mary arranged for Ciara to be allowed into the Intensive Care Unit and for her to be alone with her brother, as it was in his best interest. Ciara was unable to look at him until they were alone and then she cried at the sight of the man she loved, looking helpless in the bed and all the equipment that surrounded him.

Approaching the bed slowly, she took his hand and bent down to kiss it. She called his name softly at first, then a little louder. David didn't respond at first, then she felt slight pressure on her hand. She thought she saw the beginnings of a smile, but it could be her imagination because that was what she wanted more than anything. The nurse was far away enough that Ciara thought she could speak freely to David, and she did.

Holding his hand firmly, she began. "David, I thought I would never see you again. It looked like the world was against us from that first night onwards, but here we are. Now you just have to wake up. Please wake up, David. You have a big job to do. We have to be here for our baby. It was the last thing on my mind the night we made love, but David, you are going to be a father." Seeing the irony of that, Ciara giggled. "A dad, David. That is what you will be. Can you hear me?" This time she was not mistaken, he did squeeze her hand. Her first inclination was to call the nurse, but this was their time, and they had an awful lot to talk about. She was staying with him until they made her leave.

"Now I know that you can hear me. Are you happy that you are going to be a dad? Come on David, let me know. Squeeze twice for yes, once for no." He said yes, he squeezed her hand twice! The tears that came now were tears of pure joy.

"Do you want to see your family?" One squeeze. Ciara laughed. "Do you want me to stay here?" Two hand squeezes. He answered yes. "Ok then, try to say my name." This didn't happen. Perhaps yes and no was enough for now. "You rest now, my love." It was good to just sit and stare at him. She lifted his hand and put her one under it, then put her other hand on her tummy, as if connecting the three of them. They were a family now, and soon he would be able to feel his child move.

A nurse came to check on David and asked Ciara to step outside. She was surprised to find his parents sitting there, waiting for her to come out. When the nurse was finished, she called Mr and Mrs Magee, and there was no time to say goodbye to him. Close to tears at having to leave him, Ciara walked to her car before she cried. Her heart was breaking at having to drive away from David and the hospital, not knowing when she would see him again.

Mary was at the house when she got home and saw Ciara's face red and swollen from crying. Mary Magee hugged, her tight. "Come on now. I think it's time we had a good chat. I have had my suspicions for a while now, but I need to know about you and my brother." Mary put the kettle on.

Ciara began the story. She finished my saying how David had squeezed her hand and understood what she was saying. They both laughed now.

"I'm going to be an auntie. Oh Ciara, I'm delighted! Do you know what it is? A boy or a girl?"

"No, it's too early to tell at this stage, but I am due for a scan. Do you want to come with me, Mary?" asked Ciara.

"Yes, I would love to. Better not mention it to my mother yet. She still thinks he will go back to the church!" said Mary.

Chapter 35

Monday morning and everything was looking good from Ciara's point of view. David was recovering, and he loved her. It was time for her scan. Mary came to collect her and take her to the hospital. Kate made her promise to ring her as soon as she was done with the scan. When they got to the hospital, Mary said that she would look in on her brother before they went to the scan. As she was about to enter the ward, she heard voices. One was clearly her mother, and the other was a man, a priest. She could hear Mrs Magee say, "You are right Father, without the church, my son has no home and no job. Being a priest is his life, and we must do our best to get him back to his calling." Mary moved back from the door, in shock at her mother's words. Surely, their mother knew that David meant what he said about leaving the church.

It was better not to say anything to Ciara right now. They would continue as planned, and she would sort her mother out later. Mrs Magee was a strong-willed woman and was used to getting her own way. But by God, thought Mary, not this time.

Mary remembered how her mother had steered David into the priesthood, from the time he was a young boy. He grew up thinking that the church was his calling, his only option. Religion was a big part of their family, and on Sunday morning after mass, they would discuss the gospel and what the priest spoke about. Most of it went over Mary's head, but her mother was not directing it at her daughter. Her son was going to be a priest.

David was a grown man and had made his decision. He would get her full support. She would do whatever it took. Even if that meant going firmly against her mother, not something she ever thought she would have the courage to do.

This scan was very different for Ciara because circumstances had changed, and her baby's auntie was with her. As the technician prepared Ciara, Mary held her hand. Both women were a bit surprised at not being able to see a tiny baby, but the technician pointed out, the little heartbeat and assured them that the next time they would have more to see, but for now, all was well. Ciara was happy.

Mary, on the other hand, knew that she had a battle to fight to save her brother from the clutches of the church. She would go straight to him now and take

Ciara with her. She would tell them the whole story if she had to. When they entered David's room, they were shocked to find that he was not there. A nurse was clearing out the room. When Mary asked where her brother was, the nurse explained he has been taken to a hospital in Cork for recuperation and physiotherapy. It has been organised by the church.

The nurse smiled and said, "Don't worry, Father Magee is in the best of hands. Otherwise, the doctors would not have allowed him to be moved."

It was not his physical health that concerned Mary. Father David Magee was not weak-minded, but he needed to be close to Ciara now and not stuck in some sort of church prison.

Ciara couldn't believe what she was hearing. She had lost him again. Mrs Magee told her daughter that she didn't know where they had taken her son. The two women sat in the corridor at the hospital and looked at each other in desperation. Ciara had an idea. Marcus Langley. "We need to talk to Marcus. He will know what to do," she said to Mary.

The two women drove home in silence, both at a loss for words, as to how they were to rescue the man they loved.

As they turned the corner that took them to the Langley house, Ciara said, "Oh no, what the hell does he want?"

"Who?" asked Mary.

"Bill. My husband. That's him in the black jeep." Mary drove around the jeep into the driveway.

Bill was there by the car when they got out. "Well Ciara, are you ready to return home yet?" he said with a smirk on his face. Ciara couldn't think of an answer. But Bill continued. "Go on, get rid of that mistake in your belly and we'll be ok. You know you have it all with me. What have you got now, living with your sister, no income – you couldn't support that brat even if you wanted to. You won't get a cent off me, that's for sure." No one noticed Marcus standing in his doorway.

Ciara found her voice and let him have it. "Actually Bill, you might well be helping me to raise this child. David is suing you for defamation of character. And I will be looking for a healthy settlement in the divorce court."

He threw his head back and laughed. "Some hope. Your cripple of a boyfriend made you pregnant while being a priest. You won't find a solicitor to take on the case, let alone win."

Ciara was taken aback for a moment until Marcus joined the conversation. "You are wrong there, Bill. We already have a barrister waiting to make the case. Get back in your fancy car, get out of here and don't come back. We'll see you in court."

Marcus put his arm around his sister-in-law and led her inside. Mary followed them.

"Thank you, Marcus," Ciara said as she plopped into the first chair available.

Chapter 36

"Marcus, are we really going to take him to court?" asked Ciara.

"Yes, we are or at least you are, and so is David."

For the first time in a while, all three had a good laugh. It was Mary who got back to reality first saying, "Yes, he has to be held accountable for what he did to David." Turning to her friend she said, "Ciara, I didn't like to say anything until now, but having seen him in action, he must pay for what he did to my brother."

"Let's not forget that he also married you under false pretences, Ciara. Remember he did admit that the night he came here. We can talk to our solicitor about that too, but first, we have to find David." Mary had told Marcus about how they had taken David to another hospital and would not say where that was.

"I will find out where he is later, and I will ring you, Mary. The church cannot keep him prisoner as far as I know," said Marcus.

The pure joy of seeing her baby earlier in the day was now almost forgotten. Ciara was feeling tired and worn out. This was not how she imagined her first pregnancy in all the years of dreaming about it. Almost falling into the sofa and put her feet up, the urge to sleep took over and was barely aware of a blanket being placed over her. As she drifted to sleep, Ciara was grateful that Mary Magee was there with her, making her feel connected to David.

That evening James Bowe, the solicitor called to the house. After dinner they all sat around the kitchen table and filled him in on what had been happening.

He started with a letter to Bill informing him that a case was going to be taken against him for slandering Father David Magee. Then there was the fact that David had decided to leave the church and presumably he had written a letter to that effect. That letter would have to be found, as this would be time-sensitive with regards to him leaving the church. Last but not least, Ciara wanted a divorce – before her baby was born, if at all possible.

They now knew where David had been moved to and that his condition had not changed. It was decided that Mary would travel to Cork the next day with James. They would also call to see the bishop and try to find out who had made the decision to move David to the new facility.

Mary was very nervous about meeting with the bishop. She knew from her own job that going against the catholic church was not easy. They did not like to be questioned, but this was for her brother, and she would do whatever it took. He had a chance of a life with Ciara and their child, a healthy life, not the one her mother had picked for him. Thank God for the solicitor at her side.

She need not have worried. James took control and insisted that they speak with the bishop. He got answers to all his questions and found that the church was looking after David's welfare. James then requested to see the letter that David had written to the bishop, informing him of his intention to leave the ministry.

Ciara could see a change come over the older man's face. "How do you know about that?" he said, raising his voice.

James was calm as he answered. "He discussed his intention with family and friends before the accident."

The bishop stood up went to a filing cabinet and produced the letter, for inspection. "Father Magee is still a member of the church."

As if not hearing him, the solicitor cut in. "I need a copy of that letter, if you please, and your signature on there also." James continued to make notes and the bishop was furious. He was not used to being treated with such disrespect.

"I need to know where David Magee is at the present time. Miss Magee and I will go to see him." They were about to leave when James turned once more to the bishop and caught him off guard. "We may need you in court when we take a case to clear David Magee's name. As you know, he was falsely accused of being a paedophile." James smiled for the first time since they entered the office. "Thank you, Bishop, for all your help. I will be in touch." Mary just nodded her head as they left.

Chapter 37

Back in the car, Mary relaxed and said, "Oh my God, how did you do that? I would have been terrified of him."

James laughed. "In my job you cannot be intimidated by people like him. That was just the start. We also have to deal with Mr Parrish. He will have a lot to say for himself and to say about David and Ciara. Now on to see your brother."

Mary rang Ciara to fill her in on what had happened with the bishop but got no answer. She put her phone away and said to James, "I will ring her later. How did you know that the bishop had a letter from David?"

"I didn't. I was bluffing, but if I had asked if he had it, he probably would have said no. According to Canon Law, the church has to receive his letter within a specific time frame."

Mary was impressed and felt sure now that James Bowe was the right person to help her brother.

Ciara was sitting in the chair, afraid to move until her sister got there. She got such a shock when she saw blood and was terrified that she might be losing her baby. Kate was calm when she arrived. "Don't worry, this happens a lot and doesn't necessarily mean anything bad. Now let's get you to the hospital."

They were halfway to the hospital when Ciara remembered that she had forgotten her phone. Kate told her to reach into her bag and use her phone. Kate wanted to ask her to forget David for the moment, but she also knew that was not going to happen, and keeping her calm now was most important.

"Hello Mary, Ciara here. I left my phone at home and am using Kate's for the moment. Are you with David yet?"

"No, but we are well on our way to Cork. Are you ok?" said Mary.

"Not sure yet. I am going to the hospital now. I am bleeding," said Ciara.

Mary had no idea what to say. "Is it serious?"

"I don't know yet. Will you ring me when you see him? Please, Mary?"

"Of course, I will. Now don't worry. Ciara, David is in good hands with James."

Ciara was also in good hands. It helped that her sister and brother-in-law worked at the hospital. First, they did a scan and then she was seen by a gynaecologist, who asked if she was under pressure or worried about anything. Not knowing where to start, Ciara felt the urge to shout at him and use language that would make her sound crazy.

"Worry is all I do, from morning until night," she answered quietly.

"Well, young lady, it has to stop for you to deliver a healthy baby. Your blood pressure is high, and I would like you to stay here for a few days to allow us to monitor you."

For Ciara, this was the last straw.

The doctor went out to talk to Kate about having her sister admitted for at least three days. Sitting there in a bed, thinking about her baby, its father and her responsibility to try and stop worrying. If only she could see him, even for a short time, it would make all the difference. Then Kate entered the small room followed by Marcus, which surprised Ciara.

It was Marcus who seemed to be in charge now. "Come on Ciara, out of that bed. We are going for a spin."

As she was getting out of the bed, the doctor came back in and stood at the end of it. "Mrs Parrish, I am releasing you into the good hands of my colleague, Mr Langley, who is taking time off to make sure that you and your baby are well taken care of."

As she walked to the front entrance with Marcus, she wondered where Kate was, but then she saw her. Kate was on her phone, she signalled to them to go to the car. Ciara was relieved to be out of the hospital bed. She totally forgot what Marcus had said about going for a spin. When her sister got into the front seat of the car, she turned around to her sister and said, "I have just spoken to Mary. She is with David, and we are going to Cork now."

There were two pairs of eyes on her now, and all she could say was. "Thank you." She rubbed her stomach gently and quietly spoke to her baby. "We are going to see your daddy."

Chapter 38

The clinic looked more like a hotel than a hospital. They were met by a staff member and taken straight to where David was being cared for. They were all surprised to find Mary with James sitting outside the door. Mary had her head in her hands. James saw them approaching and went to talk to Marcus. The look on Marcus Langley's face frightened Ciara. Mary tried to smile, but it was evident that she had been crying.

Going straight to Mary, Ciara said, "What's wrong? Is he alright?"

"I don't know. I was talking to him when something happened. I think he has had a seizure of some sort. The consultant is with him now."

Kate signalled Marcus to go in and talk to the doctors. The rest of them sat down to wait, not knowing what to expect. James sat next to Mary and put his arm around her shoulders, not a word was uttered between them. They seemed to have been there for an hour when Marcus finally came out the door. His face told them that David was alive. There was relief in the air as Marcus told them that David did have a minor seizure, and it has passed.

"Come and have some tea or coffee. We will know more shortly. They will come and get us as soon as possible," said Marcus.

Ciara didn't want to leave, but her sister forced her off the seat. "Come on, sis. You can do nothing here. Think of the little one inside you. David will be ok. I just know he will."

Ciara looked at her sister. "Kate, I don't know how much more I can take." Tears were flowing down her cheeks. "If I lose him, I can't go on."

It was time for the older sister to take charge. "Stop it, Ciara. You are here and will see him shortly. Now calm down."

Mary sat beside Ciara and began to tell her about the visit to the bishop when they were interrupted by a woman who appeared to be a doctor. "Who is Ciara?" she asked, they all looked in her direction as Ciara stood up. "You need to come with me." The woman gave no explanation, and no one asked for one. As the two women walked away, the others looked from one to the other. It was Mary who spoke first. "Why did she ask for Ciara? How did she know her name?"

David was lying in a bed. There were no tubes. He was smiling. Ciara rushed to his side and kissed him full on the lips. The doctor then introduced herself and sat down. "Hold on now, you two," she said with a massive smile on her face. "You will have to take it slowly." Ciara was holding his hand and barely listening to the doctor. She had waited a long time for this, but now she had to know where they went from here. The doctor stood up. "I feel like I am wasting my time trying to talk to you two! I will go out to your friends and make plans for the immediate future." She left the room, laughing out loud. It was cases like this that made her work so rewarding.

She sat at the table with the others and explained how well David was doing and asked how they wanted to go from here. Kate and Marcus assured her and Mary that David could come to stay with them for as long as he wished to.

After the doctor had left, James Bowe took Marcus aside and filled him in on his meeting with the bishop. He also said that he would be getting back to Bill Parrish, and hopefully get a full apology and a reasonable settlement for Ciara and David to start their new life together.

Before leaving he went back to Mary. He asked her if she wanted to come back with him. Mary declined, as she wanted to be close to her brother. He then proceeded to ask her out, making it clear, that this would be a date. She said yes.

David put his finger to his lips to tell Ciara to be quiet. He caught her hand and spoke for the first time. "Did I have a dream, or did you tell me that we are having a baby?"

"Yes, my love, I did tell you that." A large smile spread across his face and tears rolled down his cheeks, and they both cried with joy. Looking upwards, Ciara said, "Thank you, God."

About the Author

This book has been a long time coming, I have always wanted to write, but life always got in the way until now. When I did start, I really liked the writing part of it, however letting someone else read it was scary. Then I asked my friend Orla Morrissey to give me her opinion. She liked it and wanted to know more about the characters and what happened to them. That is how my first book came about.

Please Review

Dear Reader,

If you enjoyed this book, I would really appreciate if you could leave a review on Amazon or Goodreads. Your opinion counts and it does influence buyer decision on whether to purchase the book or not. Thank You!

Tessa

Lightning Source UK Ltd.
Milton Keynes UK
UKHW010040210520
363570UK00001B/14

9 781912 328604